by Michael McCloskey
Copyright 2013 Michael McCloskey
ISBN: 978-1494790554

Cover art by Howard Lyon

Special thanks to Maarten Hofman, Howard Lyon, and Stephanie Zhang.

Chapter 1

Jason Yang walked into Incarnate Encounters, the seediest establishment on the frontier world of Yaal Yaalon. About half the tables were full. Jason scanned over the scene, afraid to stare too long. He saw groups of two and three, mostly men. The closest group had dirty clothing and grim faces. Builders? Miners? He could not tell. The place looked worn by his standards, but Jason had been prepared for that. It amazed Jason that even with robot workers, computer controllers and space suits, everyone on the frontier still managed to get so dirty.

Being a core worlder, he might well have been nervous in such a place, but the presence of his two bodyguards reassured him. Flanking his right was an ex mercenary named Jaxir Tortorella. On his left a humanoid security robot called Flair Five shadowed him in silence. It probably gathered a lot of attention, but Jason had been told trying to hide just would not work. The curious faces that turned to regard him as he entered indicated that was true. At least most of the gazes were brief. Jason thought the patrons probably did not want trouble from some obviously rich man with hired help.

Okay, here I am, Jason thought. *Everyone in the whole place has noticed. I should have stayed on Earth.*

Jason went to the table he had reserved with his link, but a man was already sitting there. Jason decided to roll with it. He sat down across from the man. Flair and Jaxir took the outer seats, then Jason activated the sound curtain.

"I'm Jason," he said, extending his hand.

"Carter," the man said. They shook hands. Carter's hand felt rough. Jason noticed a lot of hair on Carter's burly forearm.

"I'm glad you made it," Jason said. "I think others are coming."

1

"The meeting isn't here."

"Should we order drinks and play it easy for a while?" Jason asked.

"It doesn't matter," Carter said. "Either they're following you are they aren't."

"I see. Let's get on with it, then," he said.

Carter sent Jason a pointer to a map. The route indicator showed which exit Carter wanted to take. Apparently Jaxir and Flair got it too, since they stood up. Jason and Carter followed.

This is as subtle as an asteroid buster. At least we can talk someplace better screened from surveillance than a frontier dive with cheap sound curtains.

The noise of Incarnate Encounters faded behind him as the group walked out. They proceeded along glistening dark streets in the small frontier town. Though the tiny, distant system star was overhead, it was as dark as a Terran night on Yaal Yaalon. The only reasons the surface was not frozen was the planet's hot core, a thin crust, and a touch of Terraforming magic performed by the Space Force decades ago. The air was crisp and cold but the concrete under his thin shoes felt warm.

It was less than a kilometer to the new meeting site. They walked through two long rows of concrete buildings and came to a machine yard. The complex corpses of giant digging machines obscured the landscape.

Here we are. Stay alert, he said to Jaxir and Flair. Jason realized it was useless to tell the robot, but he treated Flair just like a human assistant. No sooner had he delivered the warning than Flair Five slumped, then collapsed. Jaxir stiffened as if hit by a stunner. He fell to one side leaving Jason and Carter the only ones standing. Jason shifted uncomfortably.

So much for my escort, Jason thought grimly. *Should have stayed on Earth, should have stayed on Earth...*

"Don't move and you won't be harmed," a voice said to his link. The owner was labeled 'SF Viridian X' in Jason's link and it had a military level authority index, which let him know that the speaker was either a hacker or a representative of the Space Force.

Jason froze. A chipped and rusted section of metal on the nearest digging machine flickered. Then it resolved into a large man who strode forward, rifle in hand. His face was covered by a combat shroud. No doubt he was reporting to friends nearby.

Jason realized he was going to have to wipe his link. He could not give PIT away.

Dammit.

Before he could prepare himself, a tiny sphere flew out of a pile of old machines toward him.

Oh no. Grenade!

Jason's heart skipped a beat. His eyes flinched.

The sphere stopped before him.

I'm still alive!

"We've got this Jason, just hit the deck, if you please," it said to his link.

"What's that!" yelled the soldier.

Jason hit the deck.

From his prone position on the warm, damp concrete he watched the soldier above him scramble for cover. The small sphere zipped off to smash into the back of the soldier's calf, causing him to fall to the ground and roll.

Shots rang out. Carter ran off.

Jason caught sight of a robot scuttling among the wrecks nearby. Then he saw another. The machines were insect-like, with weapons mounted on their backs. The shooting continued, but he could not see who was doing it in the dim machine yard.

This is crazy. The frontier really is out of control.

His doubts grew. The now-familiar mantra flew through his head again. *I should have stayed on Earth.*

Maybe the safety of the core worlds really was preferable despite the oppression?

No. This has to be done.

The sounds of combat waned. More of the short multi-limbed robots aggregated around him. Jason saw a woman in a Veer combat suit walk out into the open.

"Glad you could make it, Jason. How do you like the frontier?" Telisa said.

Thank Cthulhu, it's finally her.

Jason let his tension go down a notch.

"Glad to see you, Telisa," he said from the ground. She offered him a hand up. Jason regained his feet. "Meeting you is like stepping into an action VR."

Telisa gave a single nod. "It's all real," she said.

He was struck by her good looks. Then he saw a new scar over her left eye that continued to the top of her cheek.

Why would she let that stay there?

In an instant she assessed what he must be thinking.

"The scar reminds me of something I don't want to forget," she explained.

"Okay, but your link could—"

"Have it fixed and overlay my sight so only I could see it? No. It has to be real. Some things have to be real," she said. "I don't care if other people see it."

Jason nodded. It would not have seemed like much, but a decade ago the core worlds had gone through a major scar craze. One of the big VR stars had a scar fetish, which took off in her billions of fans. In the space of two years the fad went from trending, to extreme, to all-reaching, of course ensuring its quick burn out. Scars were way out now. Core worlders took their fashion very seriously. Jason reminded himself that Telisa was not shallow in that way. If she wore a scar it was for real personal reasons and not for something transient.

"I hope it won't be so cloak and dagger for long," Jason said, shifting the conversation back on track.

"The cloak and dagger is just starting. But we'll muddle through," she said.

"Nice to see you again, Jason," Siobhan said. Jason spotted her walking across the dark yard toward him.

"And you. Incarnate, even," Jason said, smiling. He remembered recruiting Siobhan well, though he had not heard anything from her since. He tilted his head up a fraction to greet her.

She's an Amazon. And a beauty as well.

Jason could not help but hear Imanol's nickname for her in his head: Fast and Frightening. He looked back at his bodyguards. They were not moving.

"What about Jaxir and Flair Five?"

"Pay Jaxir off and release him," Telisa said. "We'll give… Flair Five? We'll give it a once over and if it's clean you can keep it."

"Okay… will do."

Siobhan rolled Jaxir onto his back and tilted his head as Jason had seen medical responders do on Earth. Jason paid off the mercenary's contract in a few seconds. He had already noticed that link services were very sparse out on the frontier. There were only a few dozen he could see at his current location. His PV warned that the emergency response latency had fallen into the red zone; out here it would take *minutes* to get an ambulance.

"Did you get the array set up before you left?" asked Telisa. She asked it like small talk, as if she knew the answer.

"Yes. But I can't guarantee the security of the array," Jason said. "Obviously," he added, looking at the downed man before him. Siobhan secured the soldier's hands, indicating he still lived.

Telisa nodded. "They can listen in all they want. We just need to be able to scan for Trilisk signs if any of them manage to escape our grasp."

"Ah, so that's what it's for! Of course, I've been wondering. But... there are Trilisks on Earth?"

"Yes. We're coming to take them down."

Jason felt a sense of awe.

Take down Trilisks?

"The Space Force may get in your way..."

"Yes. But they're controlled by the Trilisks. We'll have to deal with them and do as little damage as we can. There will probably be casualties. I give you my word I don't take that fact lightly."

Defeat the Space Force? Everyone I know thinks I work for an ordinary travel agency.

"Now what?" Jason asked. His voice betrayed his nervousness.

"Time for the real meeting. I'll do the talking," Telisa said.

Jason nodded.

Good. Very, very good. I'll just listen and try to look tough.

"Should I know who we're meeting?"

"The UED."

Jason froze. Telisa watched him.

I thought we defeated them. And with good reason...

"Uhm, you promise this is really about Trilisks?"

"Yes. I'm not here to take over Earth. We're here to save it."

Jason nodded. Working for Parker Interstellar Travels had never been anything but great for him. Now, he wondered if he had been employed by criminals the whole time. Or worse: aliens plotting to dominate Earth.

Telisa stepped a bit closer. "When we get back to my ship, I give you my word I'll show you all the proof you need to eliminate every doubt," she said quietly. "You can meet an alien."

"Thanks," he said nervously.

I knew so much about what's been going on out here. But living it myself is a bit harder than I thought it would be. Though finally seeing Telisa up close is… motivating. She's as beautiful as ever, and now she has an authoritative presence.

Telisa led Jason through the scrap yard and to a frontier house. It was a squat, half-buried dwelling with short, meter-wide windows. It looked like a bunker, but Jason assumed that had more to do with the planetary conditions than any desire for increased security. The ground would provide a lot of warmth, and there was not much light to be had from making the windows any taller.

The door opened ahead of them. Jason felt a moment of unease again, but the people inside were just walking out. There was no leaping about, no weapons waving. He exhaled silently.

Two women and a man approached them in the dim twilight of Yaal Yaalon.

"Hello," one of the women said. She looked muscular. She wore some kind of black skinsuit under an extra jacket and tall boots.

No need for the jacket unless she's hiding something in it. The boots, at least, could just be something to get dirty and discard when you get back to the ship.

"Thank you for meeting with me," Telisa said.

"Your data package got our attention," the woman said.

I guess no point in introductions just for me. Or maybe Telisa doesn't know their names anyway.

"Then you know Trilisks control Earth. I intend to remove them from power."

"Ignoring the issue of its questionable authenticity, let me just ask: you need our help? As you know, we tried to defeat the core worlds already. There isn't much left, and the Space Force is stronger than ever before, preparing to fight… oh, of all things, aliens. Then you show up."

"I've brought a space fleet with me. It's more than a match for Terran warships. We need someone to step in and minimize the chaos when we chop the head off the snake," Telisa said.

The UED group looked surprised. Then alarmed.

"You do realize that everyone's been told the aliens are coming for them? Now you're going to show up with an alien fleet? The populace will never believe you're the good guys," said the woman.

"That's why we need your help."

"I'm not sure I know who's the bigger evil here. That's saying a lot, considering I fought Earth for decades. I lost family to them. But you? Who knows who you are? Maybe you're the one under alien mind control."

"We sent you our proof."

"You sent us a giant package of crazy. We have no idea if it's real."

Telisa raised an eyebrow. "Then get better advisors. AIs if you have to—"

"Yes, our experts think it's real. But they couldn't give me the one hundred percent. They said aliens with advanced technology could fake it all—weeks of video feeds, endless machine logs, and, well, the artifacts you sent us… obviously aliens could have produced those as well. So you could still be working with, for lack of a better term, 'the bad guys'."

"Our ships don't look anything like what took out the *Seeker*," Telisa said.

"Interesting you should bring that up. They destroyed the *Seeker* without your father on it, by the way," Garrison said. "You know how that looks?"

Telisa's face shifted for a second, then relaxed.

Anger? She suppressed it quickly.

8

"As soon as we've removed the Trilisks, we can hand power over to you to set up an interim government. I know you must have had dreams about doing that. I bet you even have a few details drawn up for it, back when you started the revolt and envisioned success."

"We can't support an attack on our own kind conducted by aliens. Even Earth. If what you say is going to happen, we might move in to pick up the pieces. As it is, I'm thinking about warning them you're coming."

"That would be a terrible mistake," Telisa said.

The man shrugged. "We can't help you. Not up front."

Jason shifted uncomfortably. Though he was not privy to the details of the plan, he figured failure to get an agreement could not be a good sign.

"How far away will you be? How long will it take for you to step in? We need someone in from ground zero."

"A week or more. But we have a few people around of course, keeping tabs on things."

"Now is the time for bold decisions and risks," Telisa said. "The future of our race depends on it. That's why I'm doing this. Against Trilisks, we could fail. But we have to try."

"If you're for real, I wish you luck. We won't be there when the hammer falls."

The woman turned away. The others followed. Telisa made no move to continue the conversation.

Telisa's face looked troubled. Jason wanted to say something, but nothing came to mind.

"We'll have to find someone else," she said. "Who do you think could take over?"

Jason hesitated as she put him on the spot.

"Hrm. Well, the Space Force."

"They're in control now," Telisa said.

"No, the Trilisks are," Jason said. "They're at the top. Wielding the Space Force like we use a stunner or a laser. Get rid of the Trilisks, and you still have Terrans with the training, equipment, and desire to keep the order on Earth."

Telisa absorbed that.

"We hired you because you're smart," Telisa said. "I like your thinking. We have to figure out where to cut the hierarchy and go there. Those will be the ones in charge when their superiors go missing. Let's work on fleshing out that idea. The first problem is, how do we prepare them without them calling the alarm?"

Jason had no idea.

Chapter 2

From within his huge battleship in deep space, Kirizzo studied a vast collection of information on the Terran homeworld, Earth. Of course Kirizzo had long been a student of Terrans. He had studied their behavior within their many virtual environs. Now his attention shifted to reality. He had to know specifics about the Sol System and its inhabitants aside from the race's vast shared virtual existence.

Gorgalans had a concept of adjectives, though they were attached as metadata to nouns within a statement, typically drummed out simultaneously on the back channel of legs 35 to 40 in incarnate conversation. If Kirizzo's primary channel legs tapped out the pattern for 'planet', his rear legs might well tap out the patterns for 'large, rocky, hot, *<noun delimiter>*' at the same time. Gorgalans were adept at accepting information in this way and it felt perfectly natural to follow it visually and, later in life, also with mass sense (only immature individuals needed to watch conversation with their eyes).

An executive summary of Earth in his language included adjectives like united, connected, rich, corrupt, populous (ten billion Terrans), and homogenous (no obvious alien presence). Its population was described in Gorgalan terms as shallow, frivolous, self-absorbed, VR-obsessed, and mostly enslaved (though they appeared not to know or care).

Core world Terrans were highly concerned with their appearance. Earth Terrans even more so. They wore thin coverings that flickered between brightly colored designs that varied depending upon context such as current mood, activity, or objectives. The optimal set of designs to choose was tied to fickle social data streams, and it differed between incarnate and virtual encounters. They attached great import to things of only internal significance in the social ladder. Those who could entertain the masses, whether through works of art, music, or virtual adventures were elevated in status.

The military forces of the race were a dominant minority that operated very differently. Within the Space Force, VR entertainment was rationed and used to reward incarnate performance. That performance was measured largely by computer systems that were resistant (though not foolproof) to corruption. The Terrans preferred to keep a tight rein on their machines.

Or more accurately, the Trilisks did, Kirizzo thought. How could he separate everything he had learned between the Terrans and the Trilisks? Kirizzo thought on this for a moment and decided it was goal structure that would differentiate the two species.

The Trilisks wanted to build up the Terran war machine to use it against their enemies. What did Terrans want? From seeing the PIT team work, he saw Terrans who wanted to explore and learn. But that was a tiny segment of the population. Most of the Terrans on Earth wanted only VR time to escape a mundane existence.

This had happened to Kirizzo's race as well. When VR was introduced, more and more of the race fled into virtual worlds and competitions. Unfortunately for them, that left the Vovokans in the real world with a huge advantage. The Vovokans who sharply limited their VR time eventually took over Vovok. They enslaved and sterilized the others, sharply correcting this self-limiting behavior in the race. Those who used VR to improve their incarnate lives flourished, and those who sought VR as an ends unto itself disappeared.

The Terrans had not yet experienced this revolution, most likely because of their hesitance to flip between cooperation and competition. Robotic workers provided the populace with most of what they needed, though the transition to full automation was not complete. There was still a minority with less than 40 percent VR time who had to maintain the factories, improve the VR body support modules, and watch important facilities. These and the military forces were the ones who would eventually take over and do whatever they wanted with those who could currently afford near 100 percent VR time.

Kirizzo allowed himself to be distracted by the geography of Earth. To him, the amazing part about the Terran homeworld was the lack of crust penetration. Almost everything alive lived at or above ground level. The Terrans refused to seriously dig into the planet, yet they created endless rows of squarish artificial caves above the planet's surface. If the Bel Klaven came to this planet, the extermination would occur so much faster than it had with Gorgala. Though the fragmentation forced by huge amounts of surface liquid had lessened over time, the footprints of it still remained in flora and fauna populations.

Kirizzo wondered if living above ground made Terrans so much more vulnerable that they had to extend their alliances across relatively long periods to survive. Could this simple but important environmental difference explain why Terrans lacked the Vovokan quick trigger cooperation-competition switch?

There was a lot going on in the rest of the system that would affect the PIT mission. Armadas of Terran war vessels were stationed at several points in the system, ready to intercept alien incursion. The ships were relatively small and harmless by Vovokan standards. And yet by sheer weight of numbers they could not be entirely discounted.

Kirizzo detected thousands of artificial satellites and orbital platforms ready to support the defense fleet. They held a wide array of weapons to deter the alien invasion the Terrans so feared. Kirizzo wondered if their Trilisk overlords expected an invasion to actually happen. He thought they did not, at least not until they struck their enemies first.

Kirizzo looked for discontinuities in technological levels among the defenses. He saw no such clues. The Terran's capabilities grew quickly, but they had taken no shortcuts. Had the Trilisks decided not to advance the Terran sciences in unnatural ways?

Explaining theories competed for Kirizzo's favor: The Trilisks were happy to let the Terrans advance organically? The Trilisks had hidden their real weapons well? There were no Trilisks left on Earth? The Trilisks were damaged and unable to accomplish more than this?

Kirizzo stayed rock still for days, sunk deep into a complex risk and reward analysis. When he next moved, it was with a grand plan in mind.

Chapter 3

Cilreth sat with Telisa and Jason in Telisa's lavish quarters. Telisa stared at her in that way she did when she was trying to figure out if she was Cilreth or Cilreth2.

It feels awkward sometimes, but it's a small price to pay to have my duplicate, Cilreth thought.

"I don't blame them for not taking us seriously," Jason said. "Don't be angry, but maybe it's harder for you to see because you've been out on the frontier. On the core worlds, everyone knows about the *Seeker*. Everyone has been working hard to pay the taxes for the new defense fleet. Now, they're asked to potentially betray their race on our word? Of course it doesn't work."

"We need to prove it to them without warning the Trilisks," Telisa said absently.

"Tall order. If the smoldering remains of the UED was thinking about turning us in…" Cilreth said.

"We can tell someone important right before we strike. Give them the heads up they would need to fill the power vacuum fast," Telisa said.

"A few hours lead would be great, but we still risk alerting the Space Force even with that," Jason said. "I'm not trying to be the negative one here. I want to remove the aliens from power as much as you do."

"The Trilisks. Don't forget we have Shiny, and he's on our side," Telisa said.

"Of course. I meant the Trilisks," Jason stumbled.

Shiny makes him nervous too, Cilreth thought. *Maybe they should meet. That would scare him even more at first, but over time… we don't have time.*

One of Cilreth's programs sent her an alert. She followed the pointer and saw what had been flagged. It was a news story that gave her an idea.

"I may have found a unique opportunity," Cilreth said. "It's kinda crazy, but we're about to attempt a coup on the largest, most powerful government Terrans have ever had. So crazy is in line with our current plan."

"You intrigue me," Telisa said, smiling.

Cilreth brought up the story link for them to look at.

Core World Delegation to Visit Earth Incarnate.

Cilreth continued immediately, even though the others were still absorbing it. "These are ministers from other core worlds. And I think they've sensed a change in Earth. They're coming incarnate to discuss policy decisions they don't like. They may well be walking into a Trilisk grinder."

"The battleship *Bismarck* has been assigned escort duty for the delegation," Jason said. "But I guess *Clacker* can handle even the newest of Terran warships?"

"Yes," Telisa said. "And it's even better that *Bismarck* is there. If we can convince a Space Force fleet officer of what's going on, he could help stabilize the system during the transition. Our ships are strong, but they're alien. The continued presence of alien dreadnoughts would generate anxiety and distrust, so we have to leave after the Trilisks are hit. There are some space force admirals on the list of a hundred, but with them out of the way, it might work."

"It gets better," Cilreth said. "There's an admiral on board the *Bismarck*. He's not on the list. We can check him anyway. If he's not a Trilisk host, then he could be someone that could help keep law and order in the system in the wake of our strike."

"Won't we just warn the Space Force we're doing this?" Jason said.

"Our Vovokan ships can jam their communications. Better than jamming, actually, if we want, it wouldn't even be apparent to either side for a while. And we can disable the ships without harming anyone," Cilreth said. "Of course, taking prisoners is a terrible way to make friends."

"They'll see our overwhelming superiority. And we won't board the ships," Telisa said. "They'll be super pissed, but when we remove the Trilisks and leave, then they'll know it was true. We wouldn't just show up, take out some leaders and leave unless it was real. Once they see that, we can apologize. They'll know it had to be done."

"We can use the evidence package we gave to the UED representatives," Cilreth said. "We still have a lot of stuff lying around. They may see it as fabricated, but it's hard to come up with so many details. If they have an AI, it might be able to tell it's all real."

Jason shrugged. "I wouldn't believe it. I would just assume the alien AIs are smarter than my AIs."

Cilreth suppressed her 'Diminishing Returns in Intelligence' speech. Grudgingly, she agreed with him. The evidence could always have been produced by more AIs, with more time to work on it. The element of the unknown, the mysterious source of the information, all this would work against them as it had when trying to convince the UED.

"There is, of course, the tiny problem of actually defeating the Trilisks as well," Cilreth said.

"Either we succeed or fail. We may as well plan for success. There's no reason to plan for what to do dead or enslaved," Telisa said.

"I agree," Jason said.

"We need to capture those ships, seal the communications down tight, and keep anyone from getting hurt. Can you do it?" asked Telisa.

Cilreth bit her lip. *She wants me to get Shiny's help. And by Cthulhu, she's right.*

"I think I could do it myself. But on something this important, I'd like to coordinate with Shiny on it."

Telisa nodded. "Okay. Get things ready. And please figure out how we can find and intercept the delegation. The rest of us will be preparing to hit the Trilisks, so if you can own this, it will really help."

***

Siobhan ran down the hill at full speed. Her idea of full speed outstripped the average person's; both her long stride and her fearless abandon sent her down the incline very quickly. She barreled out of control, falling as much as running. The grass on the hillside promised a soft landing but Siobhan knew from experience that crashing at this point would be bone-jarring at best. The tall clumps of grass hid logs and stones.

Caden was just ahead. His stronger, more compact body negotiated the slope with more skill yet Siobhan started to overtake him. He seemed to feel that some measure of control was needed. Siobhan did not think so.

Siobhan loped up beside him, feeling the jolt of each landing as she gathered more speed. She knew she could not keep it up much longer, but just ahead, they would run out of hill...

They ran at full speed right off the cliff.

They both screamed wildly as they hurtled downwards. To Siobhan's right, a gigantic waterfall roared down the cliff with them. As Siobhan neared the lake below, she put her legs together and spread her arms to align herself for the feet-first insertion.

The impact was brutal. Her suit did what it could to spread the impact across her legs. They both sank below the white maelstrom into a shadowy part of the lake below the fall. Siobhan's long body slid deeper into the water than her partner. Above her, Caden sped off with strong strokes toward the surface. Siobhan followed his course. They took a slight angle away from the falls.

He remembers the spot.

Siobhan felt her anticipation rise.

They broke the surface of the water and pulled in deep breaths of cool air. Caden grinned wildly at her. They swam up to a tiny beach. Caden emerged from the water slowly, stealthily. He always practiced it. Siobhan copied him.

Just past the beach was a green misty meadow. The air smelled of the electric-fresh spray of the waterfall. The foliage was thick, forming a wall all around them. Caden collapsed onto the fresh grass, still smiling. Siobhan toppled onto him like a falling tower. He let out a mock cry of alarm, then absorbed the impact.

They laughed. Then she kissed him for a long time. She pulled away and looked at his perfect face.

"Do you ever worry about what will happen to us?" she asked.

"The missions? Why worry? I know you. You won't back down."

"It's just that—maybe we don't have much time together."

He suddenly smiled wide. "If anything happens to you, I'll be your Ledoux!" He winked.

Siobhan laughed out loud. Ledoux was a main character of a well known romance-tragedy from the last century. It was set in a time before complete biological regeneration had been mastered. In the book, Ledoux, a famous cyberneticist, falls in love with a smart, beautiful woman. He adores her and always dotes on her as a very caring partner. Then she has a terrible accident, leaving her body and mind heavily damaged. Ledoux resolves to rebuild her, but the first thing he constructs is a lie detector because he wants to know for sure if she is pleased and satisfied with her new parts. He replaces her leg and she is pleased. Then he continues to rebuild her, but slowly, her satisfaction with her new life as a cyborg begins to wane, as her hope gives way to a cold reality. Ledoux monitors this with his device. He sees her becoming less happy, so he strives harder and harder to please her. Finally she is basically complete, but finds herself ostracized by her largely artificial body and troubled by the cold, artificial parts of her new mind. She tells him she is happy, but the device reveals otherwise. Having worked so hard, the obsessed and now unstable Ledoux replaces the natural part of her brain that drives her unhappiness, making her permanently content, though the last trace of the woman he had known is gone.

"I feel so much better now!" she joked back. They grinned at each other like idiots.

Siobhan's link interrupted the tryst. It said Telisa wanted to talk to her. She rolled away and stared into his eyes. Then she sighed.

"What's wrong baby?" he said. He reached out to touch her hair.

"Gotta go," she said. Siobhan deactivated the VR. The Caden simulacrum, the sun, the grass, and the mist disappeared in an instant.

Siobhan sighed. She should tell him. She knew that.

I'm not afraid to jump out of a spacecraft in the middle of a dense planetary ring, but I'm too wimpy to ask Caden if he wants to… get a little closer.

Siobhan locked up the simulation file and left it on her link. She did not trust PIT to refrain from snooping around her storage on the *Clacker*, but maybe they would at least respect the privacy of her link. As much as they complained about the UNSF violating privacy, it would be pretty hypocritical of them to go looking at her personal VR setups.

Siobhan rolled out of her huge bed on the *Clacker*. Telisa had invited her to a mess though it was not mealtime. Siobhan smiled. She was always hungry and Telisa knew it.

When Siobhan arrived incarnate, she found Telisa waiting for her. Telisa's wounded eye had a complex iris and pupil that made it obvious the eye was artificial. The scar above and below her eye remained.

"You like the scar?" Siobhan asked.

"No one else told you?"

"Told me what? I guess I don't hang out with the others as much as we used to. I mean, off training hours."

Maybe she's checking to see if her scar and eye are on the rumor mill.

Telisa nodded. "It reminds me of what happened, and what I need to do. I know it sounds dumb. It's just important to me."

"Not dumb," Siobhan said. "What's happening?"

"I have work for you," Telisa said. "Probably not your favorite but it's important. Files for you to read. Then some brainstorming and planning."

The only thing I like to plan is revenge. No, don't say that.

"Have you heard of the Orwell Papers?" asked Telisa.

"No."

"It's a plan to overthrow the UN government. The important part, we believe, is the analysis of the power structure. Almost all the power is in the hands of a hundred individuals or less. I'm betting those are where the Trilisks are hidden. So we're going after them with our fingers crossed."

"Wow! I'll read through it," Siobhan said.

Damn. That's crazy. We're crazy!

"Dangerous enough for you?" Telisa asked innocently.

Siobhan laughed. "I think it'll keep me stimulated."

"Okay, good. Absorb this material. We'll plan more later."

Telisa left Siobhan to grab some food. Siobhan dug into the information. She began to think about just how large the task before them was. Yet she knew they could do it. She gained confidence and knowledge as she made her way through it, until she reached the biographies of the top one hundred.

Siobhan's blood ran cold. She saw a name she knew. Kagan Spero.

Kagan was a powerful force in Speronautics Space Fabrication Corporation. The Spero family kept a tight rein on the oligarchical company. This was the family that had enslaved her ancestors on a space habitat.

It's probably not actually a series of family members. It's probably just one immortal Trilisk. A Trilisk responsible for it all.

Siobhan left the mess and went for a long walk around *Clacker*, burning off a surge of angry energy.

That bastard is a Trilisk. Or he works with them. He is so dead.

Chapter 4

Admiral Sager looked at his personal VR quota. He had stored up the maximum rollover hours, so if he did not find time today to use some, it would be gone forever.

I should be able to leave them to my progeny, he thought dryly. *I guess I should get some progeny before worrying about that one.*

The acting captain of the *Bismarck* spent so much time working on real world issues he barely got into personal VR anymore. Of course, that was exactly what the Space Force wanted, except when it came to training. Everyone spent a few hours training in virtual environments day in and day out.

He sat on the observation deck, even though there was nothing to see. With the gravity spinners spooled up at full power, the ship's particles were forced into tachyonic state and they had left the normal universe behind. The smooth black tables and chairs of the deck were lit through the observation portal with the cool blue flame of their gravity envelope.

The *Bismarck* had been assigned to protect a core world delegation ship carrying important leaders to Earth. Admiral Sager did not think much of the assignment, but it was better than performing endless drills around Sol. At least the *Bismarck* finally got to leave Earth. As one of the most powerful new battleships made since the alien threat had come to light, it was kept close to home. Though the *Seeker* had been an exploration vessel, it had possessed powerful weapons. Yet the aliens had apparently dispatched it easily. That terrified Earth. *Seeker*'s destruction had started a huge build up across all the Terran held worlds.

"The *Marco Polo* has detranslated," a helm officer reported on the command channel. The officer was not physically present. Admiral Sager did not inquire as to the whereabouts of the man. Anyone in navigation, or for that matter in any area of command, could perform their duty from anywhere on the ship.

Admiral Sager flipped up a nav display in his personal view. Their delegation ship had flipped from tachyonic particles into the sublight universe. Thus, *Bismarck* had left them way behind.

"Drop out and compute a rendezvous translation," Sager ordered. "Send them a t-packet and let them know we're coming."

The *Bismarck*'s gravity spinners reduced power enough for the battleship to detranslate. Once in normal space, several virtual alarms immediately activated.

"What the hell?" Sager said. Comments from other officers mimicked his own surprise. Officers all over the ship stopped whatever they were doing and furiously looked through panes of data in their PVs.

"The gravity spinners are dropping lower than we told them to," someone said.

"We have contacts on the tactical," another officer rattled off excitedly. "Two… two *absolutely huge* contacts!"

"Battlestations," Sager snapped. "Defense status five."

"Defense status five," echoed Raigel, the *Bismarck*'s tactical combat AI.

The top defense status call caused many things to happen all over the ship. Point defense weapons charged up, EM pods prepared to mitigate incoming energy, and weapons locked onto nearby contacts on the tactical. Raigel took command of large portions of the power output of the ship, using it to begin erratic maneuvers.

Sager looked at the contacts. They were alien ships. They had to be. Their size was scary. Even larger than alien ships had been in the virtual drills they had conducted.

This is real, he had to remind himself. The situation was like so many that had come up in virtual training since the alien threat had appeared. Except the situation was even more dire than some of their doomsday scenarios. *And this is it. We're dead.*

"Raigel," Sager addressed his combat AI. "You're authorized to do whatever it takes. If we can't win, we have to warn Earth."

"Understood," Raigel responded. The voice sounded synthetic as required by UN law, just as the name of an AI had to include the sequence "ai". Core world citizens demanded that it be obvious when they were dealing with an artificial mind.

"Communications penetration: zero," reported Raigel. "We cannot contact the *Marco Polo*, either. Enemy ships register on visual wavelengths only."

"Visual only? How is that possible?"

"They demonstrate we can see them only because they allow it," Raigel surmised. "It is an intimidation tactic."

"Can we fight our way out?" asked Sager's second, Captain Narron. Sager saw Narron had joined him on the deck. The captain hurried over to his side.

"Weapons will be ineffectual," Raigel said. "More analysis is required, but I believe this is checkmate."

Narron leaned forward. "I think Raigel has been compromised."

"Raigel, explain," Sager said.

"Many of our systems are under heavy enemy influence, including the gravity spinners and our power plants," Raigel reported. "The objects we detect on visual wavelengths are most likely not where they appear to be. If our weapons do even fire, they will be firing off target."

The most powerful battleship ever made, and we're defeated before even firing a shot.

"If it's not real, then their size and appearance can be faked, too," Narron said. "Maybe the enemy ships aren't large at all. Maybe there's only one."

"Distract them," Sager said. "Target our energy weapons at the most likely locations for enemies. Launch missiles and put them on standby patrols. Launch all our courier ships with warning messages, have them translate to FTL. Maybe…"

"We're receiving a transmission most likely from the aliens. Continue with your orders?"

"Wait," Sager said.

"They know our protocols, too?" Narron asked.

"Affirmative. Routing the channel through to you," Raigel said.

A woman's face appeared on the screen. She was attractive, though with a scar across her left eye socket and an obviously artificial eye.

There's no reason to have a scar and such a gaudy eye. She wants us to see that for some reason, Sager thought. *Another intimidation tactic? Seems kind of juvenile.*

"I'm sorry for disabling your ships. Earth is under threat," she said. She pursed her lips, took a breath, and continued. "I'm going to lay it out for you straight. We have a fleet of alien ships and we're headed for Earth. But we're not the force that destroyed *Seeker*. We're here to remove an alien influence from the top echelons of Earth's government. We've chosen to isolate you because we want to win over your support. Or at the very least, prepare you to take over when we leave. Earth will be leaderless as a result of our action."

"The person portrayed is a good facsimile of Telisa Relachik, the child of Captain Relachik of the *Seeker*," Raigel said on the officer channel.

"The kid of Relachik? Sick joke. These aliens are twisted," said Narron.

Sager looked at the channel from the aliens. It was set up for two way communication.

"Show yourselves. Release my spinners, and we will negotiate with you," Sager said on the channel.

"As I said. I have to isolate you. I can't let the aliens know I'm coming. I don't expect you to understand or believe me now."

"What have you done with *Marco Polo*?"

"It will be joining you shortly," the woman said. "I suggest you move that delegation aboard *Bismarck*, Admiral Sager. Just in case things get really ugly. The survivability of the delegation should improve on that battleship. These core world politicians will be useful in lending weight to your claim to power under martial law when we leave."

Sager shook his head. It was all too much to believe. *They could just destroy us if they wanted. Could it be real? They know who I am.*

The woman stared at them in silence for a moment more. "I have evidence to offer you," she finished. "I'll arrange for its delivery. I want you to get looking at it right away, and I know you'll fear a hack. So, I'm going to disarm your point defenses now just to show you that I can."

"Point defenses have deactivated," Raigel said.

"I don't need to hack you. I can set any bit in any system on the ship from here," she said. "So do Earth a favor and take a look at my evidence, think about my plan, and make plans of your own. Earth will be leaderless within the next few days. The *Bismarck* will be an important part of keeping things together."

The channel closed.

"We have received a large data package," Raigel said. "The *Marco Polo* has detranslated within ten thousand kilometers of our position."

"Raigel, figure out how to detect them. Send the package over to Daimyo for analysis," Sager ordered, trading glum looks with Captain Narron.

Chapter 5

Caden had just finished a hard workout with a training android. He sat breathing deeply on a Jiu Jitsu mat, feeling the new abrasions and bruises scattered over his body. He would never trade in all his real workouts for virtual ones. Even though he could only try out the most dangerous things in the VRs, he was training for real action now. Besides, the endorphin rush was priceless. There were pills for that, but what good would they be when he was fighting for his life on some alien planet?

"Caden," Telisa sent him.

"Here," he said.

"Important meeting. We have something new cooking," Telisa said. She was all business. She had not cracked a smile since losing Magnus.

"On my way," he said. Caden hopped into a shower tube for ten seconds to clean up, then tossed on a change of clothes. Being in a hurry, he headed out with a shock of wet hair, wearing only a pair of loose trousers and a short sleeve shirt. The shirt did not change colors like a colorweave, but neither would it fall apart if he had to dive and roll or climb down a cliff.

Siobhan intercepted him on the way to the meeting. Her eyes flickered down, taking in his mussed appearance.

She's checking me out!

He smiled at her.

"Hi," she said. She smiled at him for one second, then looked away.

"Hey. Do you know what's up?"

"Nope. Just been training," Siobhan said.

Caden nodded. Siobhan acted a bit odd sometimes. She often smiled and chatted, but then she seemed to want to bug out quickly.

She's from a different place with different customs, he reminded himself. Still, he had the most in common with

29

Siobhan. He remembered all the fun they had had jumping around in the Blackvine habitat. Caden and Siobhan were the youngest, and like Telisa, they were adventurous.

"We could go jump around a sim of that habitat after the meeting," Caden said suddenly. "You know—the Blackvine houses in the sky."

"What! Oh! Yes, that would be cool," Siobhan said.

"Okay then, it's a date."

Siobhan's eyes bulged.

Oh. She's freaked out because I said 'date'.

"Not a *date* date I mean. Oh, we don't have to if you don't wanna," Caden said.

"I want to," she said quickly.

They walked into big room on the *Clacker* for the FTF. Caden saw both of the Cilreths, Maxsym, and Imanol.

"Wunderkind and Fast'n'Frightening," Imanol said. "Nice of you to drop by. You guys having a little FTF of your own? Or maybe I should say BTB?"

Body to body. As in, incarnate.

Caden let the remark slide right off. Telisa and Cilreth would see he may be younger than Imanol, but he acted more professionally day in and day out. Siobhan decided to strike back.

"You could have had some incarnate time with me too, Imanol," Siobhan said sweetly. "Oh that's right. You're *afraid* of me."

"No, that was GI Jane."

The remark caught Caden off guard. Leave it to Imanol to mention Arakaki. Caden knew if she had been at the meeting, she would ignore it. So Caden did too.

Okay, I officially hate this jerk. He doesn't know where to draw the line.

"As you may be aware," Telisa started in, "We're going to stop the Trilisks that rule Earth. I have a group preparing to take over after we're done. We just go in and

30

find the Trilisks. We'll take them out with minimum engagement with the Space Force."

Caden's eyebrows lifted. Imanol looked equally surprised, though Maxsym and Siobhan remained placid.

A new channel opened with a data stream describing a space habitat. Caden looked it over in his PV. Skyhold. He had heard of it. It was supposed to be a really important space habitat.

"We've discovered that Skyhold is home to over eighty percent of our targets," Telisa said. She let that sink in while everyone looked Skyhold over.

"It's tempting to assume that all the Trilisks are together there," Siobhan said. "Maybe the others are just Trilisk sympathizers, or... just power hungry people who don't know who their allies really are?"

"The same thought occurred to me," Telisa said. "But we can't assume it. I don't know enough about Trilisks to know if they would prefer to segregate themselves, even in human form."

"Maybe they take other forms there, and no one is around to see," a Cilreth said.

"Then one of us goes ahead to figure out what's going on," Caden said.

"The security is insane there," the other Cilreth said. "The habitat itself carries as much armament as a Space Force cruiser. Internally, there's a strong robotic security force controlled by multiple AIs."

"Sounds like a target for *Clacker*'s main weapons," Caden said. "Take them all out in one shot."

"Maybe. We have to verify they're actually Trilisks," Telisa said.

"There are others on that station. Servants," a Cilreth said.

"Slaves!" Siobhan said. "You can bet on it. Those 'servants' are slaves."

She said something about her family being slaves, Caden thought.

"I'll go in and scan them," Caden said. "I can let you know, get out, and we can let them have it! If there's a mix of targets and noncombatants there, then we need a more complicated plan B."

"Thanks for the offer, but I have another mission for you, Caden," Telisa said.

Really? She already has a mission for me?

"What?" Caden said.

"Space Force Command," Telisa said.

What!

No one dared speak for a moment. Everyone stared at him.

"There's a Trilisk…?" he asked.

"Three people on the list. Two men and one woman. Admirals. They're likely Trilisks in my opinion. If you were setting up the Space Force as a tool to do your bidding, this is where you would be."

Caden bristled at the thought.

Wow. I've got to weed them out! We can't have aliens in control of the Space Force!

"Security would be tight," Caden said slowly. But he thought something else.

If I got rid of those aliens, they'd have to let me in. I could still be an officer.

"It's not lost on me that you planned to join the Space Force, Caden," Telisa said. "Here's your chance to be their hero. Though they won't know that until we're done. We have to figure out how to get you, or at least an attendant sphere in there and scan those people. If they're Trilisks, we have to take them out. And we won't be able to use the orbital weapons or the *Clacker* to do it. We can't open fire on Space Force Command. We have a lot of planning to do. I'll be coordinating with all of you separately. We're taking a hiatus from our group training, because we all need to start working simulations of our individual missions."

Telisa sent Caden a copy of the Orwell Papers. Caden had already read them. They were famous. The Space Force had studied them carefully and put several safeguards into place to ensure the plan could never succeed. Telisa seemed to know that, but she considered the information valuable since it gave clues about who the Trilisks might be.

The meeting broke up and Caden headed off with Siobhan.

"I guess we can't do the jumping around right now," he said. "We have a lot of sims to set up. I want to do a lot of practice runs around a virtual command center."

Siobhan nodded. "I have work to do, too."

They split up to head to their own areas of the ship. Caden had his own room set up like a modern strongpoint, with robots guarding the door and a laser emitter embedded in the ceiling.

Maybe I can take a break later and hang with Siobhan.

***

Siobhan felt a bit depressed as she left Caden after the meeting. But she knew there were huge things ahead of them. How could she be feeding her silly crush on Caden when they needed to be saving Earth?

And I need to get my revenge.

Siobhan started to investigate the Spero family's current whereabouts on Earth. They were fairly famous, and so there was a lot of information to sift through. She finally zeroed in on Kagan in particular, and found out he was considered a recluse who spent most of his time on a tropical island compound owned by SSFC.

Siobhan made queries about the compound. She wanted the blueprints so she could formulate some plan of attack.

Theoretically such a query could be flagged and tracked, but Shiny had assured the PIT team that he knew how to obfuscate the trail of their interactions with the Terran networks. It was the only way Telisa could stay online without being tracked by the UNSF.

Her investigation found a lot of material. She copied it to her link. She brought up the building plans of the estate.

"How accurate are these, I wonder?" she asked herself quietly. "Total fabrication? That's how I'd do it if I were a paranoid immortal. Put a death trap where my bedroom is supposed to be."

Siobhan looked through the construction records. She spotted another large contract with a security company.

That's a lot of money. No doubt they're making extensive security modifications to the house. All paid for by the company, of course.

Siobhan started to get angry thinking about it. Kagan had been living in luxury while her kind suffered. He had used the labor of company employees, and even slaves, to increase his own wealth.

"You may have all your money, and your scary company, but I have more at my disposal than you do now," she muttered. But she did not have enough information to know what modifications had been made. The floor plan itself could even be altered. Or an entire new floor could have been put in for that kind of money. She frowned and leaned back on her bed, frustrated.

"Cilreth?"

"Hi. What's up?"

"One of the Trilisks is living in this heavily modified estate," Siobhan sent Cilreth a pointer. "I want to know—"

"You want to know what it looks like today."

"Exactly."

34

"I can do it," Cilreth said. "What's in it for me?"

What? She never said that before.

"Well, uhm," she stuttered.

The safety of Earth? Was she from Earth again?

"Let me make it easy for you," Cilreth said. "Next time we vote to see if Cilreth2 goes on ice, you vote no."

Aha.

"Deal," Siobhan said.

"You'll have your info within 24… minutes!" Cilreth said.

"Thanks."

Siobhan was happy to make the deal. She still only asked for connections to their original Cilreth, though. She did not like the new one on some level she had not pinned down. Maybe it was some instinct that here was an unfairly superior competitor, or the knowledge a Trilisk could take her over at any time.

Okay, so my plan is in motion. But I need Telisa to buy into it. How should I sell it to her?

Siobhan started to think up a story, but then decided against it. Telisa had been a straight shooter with her, why not show her the same respect in return? Just come out and say it. Siobhan felt that Telisa might back her.

Siobhan got up and preened herself just a bit. She felt that a conversation this important should be incarnate. She sent a message ahead asking for an FTF.

She walked out and headed to Telisa's rooms, thinking over what she would say. Telisa approved the meeting as Siobhan walked. She eventually arrived at a door mapped as Telisa's private territory aboard the vast decks of the *Clacker*.

The metal door slid open and Telisa was standing behind it.

"Hello?" Telisa said. "Come on in."

Her wounded eye always catches my attention first no matter how many times I see it. Her face was so pretty before.

Telisa's rooms were beautiful. Siobhan had heard Telisa kept a vast workshop filled with alien artifacts she studied in her personal time. But all she saw today was a nice atrium and a small side room with drinks and a kitchenette. They sat down at the edge of the atrium. Across the way Siobhan saw a statue of Magnus. She looked away quickly and pretended not to notice.

"I want to go after a particular Trilisk," Siobhan said. "I have business with one of these targets."

"Which one?"

"Kagan Spero. I want him. I want that one."

And I don't care if the frackjammer is a Trilisk or a Terran.

"Oh. Spero. I've been so busy I didn't notice that one… yah, okay, you got him."

"Thank you, Telisa. I won't forget this."

"You know where he is?"

"I think so, and Cilreth is searching up some details for me."

There was a delay.

Telisa must be doing some digging herself.

"That place is a fortress. We may have to just destroy it with a Vovokan weapon."

"No. There are other people in there. Even if all his Spero people are despicable, there will be slaves there, too."

Telisa took a deep breath. Siobhan knew what was coming.

"Believe me, I've lost sleep over this already and I haven't even hurt people like this yet. But we can't overthrow the Trilisks without hurting… without killing some innocent people. It just doesn't work like that."

Telisa looked like she was going to cry. Siobhan saw the depth of her pain.

Even if we succeed, she'll be torn apart by guilt.

"The way I see it, I won't feel guilty as long as I did what I had to do, but I took every effort possible to save as many as I could," Siobhan said. "And that means going in and taking that bastard out with precision. If I fail, then call in the artillery. That way, I can live—or die—with whatever happens."

"You'll just die. Going up against a Trilisk by yourself?"

"Well, I thought that was the plan anyway? We have to take them out. I can use some of Shiny's toys, too," she said.

"Maybe," Telisa said. "Make a plan. Let me know," Telisa said.

Siobhan left Telisa's rooms with a new mission in her heart. But it was not a new mission at all. It was the old mission, the one she had worked toward before she had discovered Parker Interstellar Travels.

Revenge.

She wanted to share her new excitement with someone.

Cilreth? Cilreth, and… Cilreth2. Hrm.

She stopped to think for a moment.

Caden.

She immediately felt nervous. Caden looked so perfect, and he was famous. How could she just saunter in and chat with a VR star?

He can't possibly like me… I'm taller… my arms and legs are so long and clumsy, and he's so graceful. Strong and dreamy.

Siobhan cursed at herself. How could she be afraid to do something *so safe*?

I'd rather climb into a missile tube and plunge into a star.

Siobhan started to walk toward Caden's quarters. She looked down at her long legs eating up the ground with giant strides and tried to think of what to say.

He's all ripped up over Arakaki's death. He said she saved him. Maybe they were even lovers.

Abruptly Siobhan chickened out. She turned away.

Shiny.

She had never tried talking with Shiny much. Telisa seemed to adore him.

"Shiny?" Siobhan asked over her link.

"Significant fraction, portion, division of attention allocated to Siobhan."

"What? Oh. Uhm, I am going to go and try and kill a Trilisk. Or a Terran. I need to kill someone."

There was a long pause. At first, she thought she had lost whatever fraction of attention Shiny had given her.

"Purpose?"

"Revenge!"

"Proposal?"

"I need some kick ass Vovokan tech to make sure I succeed. I have to kill this Terran. There's bad blood between us. Do you know what that means?"

Of course, he can just look it up if he doesn't.

"Shiny equips Siobhan for assassination, termination, murder."

"Yes! Please?"

"Delineate return offer."

"What?"

"Describe Siobhan's payment offer?"

Oh. He's asking 'what's in it for me'.

"I don't know. I don't have much. The Terran I want to kill may be a Trilisk host. Your enemy, right?"

"Offer under consideration."

Is that lack of enthusiasm normal for a Vovokan?

"And I could owe you one."

Her offer sounded lame to her own ears. There was another pause.

"Agree, accept, deal."

Michael McCloskey

Chapter 6

Maxsym completed his project only days after the meeting. He felt a flush of pride.

Not many could have done this. Though part of the credit belongs to the Clacker and the Trilisk AI.

Maxsym had always been smart. Brilliant, some had said. But the pace of his innovation had always been stifled by analyses that took days, rules that stood in his way, and bureaucracy that was even worse. Not so on the *Clacker*.

Once Shiny and Cilreth had given him a start on the computers and allowed him to use a few prayers to the AI, he had found an amazing depth of chemical simulations. The virtual environments of the Vovokan ship could watch every molecule of a developing egg and speed up its hatching to a fraction of a second. He could run entire generations of hybrids through artificial worlds to see how they would fare. He could search through entire families of molecules and play them off against each other in virtual trials. Literally every reaction that occurred in a sample could be simulated and recorded for him to watch.

Of course all that was too much data for Maxsym to handle. But the machines around him were able to classify the reactions, give him aggregated rates of production, and show him the balance points of cyclical systems. On Earth, if Maxsym wanted to try out a crazy idea, it would take days. Here it took seconds.

Maxsym had decided to focus on something of interest to the team first. He wanted to show his thanks, and more importantly, he wanted to show them what he could do. He needed to secure his use of these resources for the foreseeable future, and that meant giving the PIT team an immediate return on their investment.

So, he dug into the biology of the Terrans-as-Trilisk-hosts. Here, he had run into a construct so complex even the tools of the *Clacker* seemed inadequate to deal with it. Maxsym knew a lot about the human body, but these hosts were improved by so much it stunned him. He could spend years studying the optimizations built into the host bodies.

Fortunately for Maxsym, it was much easier to destroy than to create. He had found what he needed.

"Telisa?"

There was a delay. Then Telisa connected.

"Hi, Maxsym. What's up?"

"I have a weapon we can use against the Trilisks."

"Wow? Really? I'll be right over."

"No need," Maxsym said. "I can brief you over the link."

Maxsym winced. *Will that insult her?*

"I mean, at your convenience, online or incarnate," he clarified.

"Oh. I would like to see it in person."

"Ah. Yes. I haven't made a deployment mechanism, so there's nothing to see. Except an invisible, odorless gas that kills Trilisk hosts. It does so very quickly—within a few seconds—and paralyzes them immediately. They wouldn't even have time to access neural interfaces, unless they have mental augmentation outside the Terran host that thinks much faster than we do."

Which they might.

"Wow! That's an amazing weapon! I had no idea you were… I didn't expect anything from you so soon. So we can gas them."

"I was thinking, specifically, we could use it on Skyhold," Maxsym said.

"Ah, of course. An isolated environment. Of course, a space habitat that size…"

"Is a huge volume of air, yes. I've already produced enough for the mission. The *Clacker* is nothing short of amazing. There's no limit to what I could accomplish here! It can record and classify a million chemical reactions in a sample and categorize them, then play them back for me. We can fabricate—"

"Yes. Tell me more about the gas, though. Focus on this task first."

"Of course. I don't know how to deploy it, though, I suspect someone else may surpass my abilities there."

"We'll do whatever it takes. Hrm. And… the effects on ordinary humans?"

"It's toxic to ordinary humans as well, I'm afraid," Maxsym said. "But a dose high enough to kill every Trilisk on Skyhold would likely only kill the weakest Terrans. Only the very young or old, in all likelihood. It depends upon individual constitution and genetic factors."

There was a pause.

I'm well aware it is suboptimal…

"Thanks for doing this. We can definitely use the option. I need to think it over."

"I understand," Maxsym said. The connection dropped.

Maxsym was left to ponder the weapon he had made, and who it might kill.

***

Telisa cradled her head in her arms and closed her eyes. She sat in her huge bedroom on the *Clacker* with the lights down. Maxsym's news should have made her feel better, but she felt more lost than before.

What are we doing?

Maxsym had given her a deadly tool to use against her enemies. Using it could cause collateral damage. How could she deploy such a thing knowing it could kill innocent Terrans on Skyhold?

This is where Magnus would tell me I have to act for the greater good, she thought. *He would say someone has to have the strength to make the hard decisions. Because the universe is a cruel place.*

But Magnus was not there. Telisa felt nothing but doubt and horror. She did not want to be the one to bring war to Sol.

I'll take the weapon in myself. Scan and identify the Trilisks. Expose as few people as I can. Put some on shuttles or lock them into isolated rooms without unfiltered air. I could identify those most susceptible and protect them somehow.

Even as she thought it she knew it was not realistic. Giving the Trilisks any warning at all, even a minute's worth, would mean probable failure of her attempt to strike them down in a lightning blow.

Is toppling the Trilisks worth the death of a kid? A grandmother?

Telisa had thought she knew the answer until she closed her eyes and envisioned people dying because of her.

Chapter 7

Kirizzo planned the invasion of Sol.

According to the huge amount of data he had collected, the defenses extended to the asteroid belt. New Space Force bases dotted the belt. There were also four large bases slightly above and below the ecliptic plane of the system to help defend Earth from threats arriving perpendicular to the plane of orbit. The bases switched sides every orbit, synchronized against each other to ensure at least one would be on each side at all times. While one pair was in the plane of Earth's orbit, the other pair were at maximum distance above and below the planetary ecliptic.

Kirizzo had seven ships to attack the Trilisks not counting the *Clacker*, which the PIT team used. Despite their size, Kirizzo could completely hide them from the Terran scanning technology by any of a number of means, from electromagnetic cloaking to hacking the Terran radar systems. The Vovokan had been lurking on the Terran network for so long, he knew more about it than the Terrans themselves. Only a handful of weak AIs stood between him and total domination of their network.

In terms of firepower, any two of his seven ships could dish out more joules than the entire Terran home fleet. His point defenses could protect him from the thousands of orbital weapons platforms, if they even saw him. Finally, his ground forces, though very limited, could handle any mission on the surface he had to issue.

The Terrans were not much of a threat. But what of the Trilisks?

The Trilisks would be impossible to defeat if they still held their legendary powers. Kirizzo did not think they still did. He believed their own war had caused them to lose a lot of their technology. Otherwise, they would openly rule the Terrans and a dozen other races, and the war would be raging with the Trilisks' enemies. That did not seem to be the case, though perhaps the Trilisks conducted war at a level so advanced Kirizzo could not even recognize it.

Kirizzo had the columns and the AI. But he feared the Trilisks might know how to access this pirated technology better than he did. He would ask the AI to reduce its range dramatically, and conduct his operations far away from Earth. He had no guess as to the range they might be able to detect and access the columns. While planning to use ask AI to hide them, another thought presented itself.

There was a Vovokan idiom which meant to turn a problem into a weapon. Kirizzo thought it might be possible in this case. If the Trilisks decided they were outmatched and wanted to flee the system, would some of them access the columns? A quick switch of bodies might prove useful. A Trilisk might seek to return to a native body if they no longer needed to appear Terran.

Then Kirizzo could blast them into atoms with a powerful explosion.

Within the bowels of the *Thumper*, new machines designs flitted across the networks. Thousands of pieces of machinery flowed to and fro through the fine sand of his distribution network. In the center of his ship, near the Trilisk columns, the pieces marched together. As the pieces joined to form larger and more complex systems, the machines working on them grew from the microscopic to the macroscopic, until finally huge cutting and lifting machines were complete.

The robotic work force then set about moving the Trilisk columns out into a series of new smaller ships— Kirizzo's deadly Trilisk traps. The ships had powerful drive systems which were really just disguised bombs. Their components were subtly designed with an eye toward generating atom-shattering explosions.

The bait columns started their move outward, though Kirizzo kept some columns back. One column in particular remained of interest to him. It had produced copies of the PIT team, and he suspected it still held complete memory of them. That bargaining tool could prove useful if his plan came to fruition.

Or if it went horribly wrong.

***

Telisa's link told her it was about time for her meeting with Shiny. She jumped up toward the ceiling and dropped her hands to the floor twenty times in a rapid cycle to increase her alertness.

I have a scheduled meeting with an alien. Think about that.

She had accomplished so much. There was just a moment of satisfaction before thoughts of Magnus returned to smash it. She saw him in her mind, thought of the bristly feel of the stubble on his face. She had often teased him about his shoddy use of depilatory, though she secretly liked the feel of it. The image faded. There was only the sense of loss.

Not now. Just work.

Shiny connected on time. Telisa sent a message.

"Hi Shiny. What do we have in terms of Terran defenses at Sol?"

Shiny provided a pointer to a large body of data. Telisa opened it within her PV. A vast map of the solar system appeared with Space Force bases and ships marked in red. Telisa rotated it and zoomed in on one in the asteroid belt. A force of thirty ships were stationed there, with another two under construction in an automated factory.

Thirty ships out of a total of… *four hundred* deployed around Sol.

"We've been busy back home," she said. "Any signs of Trilisk improvements?"

"Technological development, breakthrough, innovation curve strong, shaped, accelerated. Possible drivers: mass xenophobia, alien artifacts, Trilisk influence, increased use of artificial intelligences."

"Can you handle everything without hurting anyone?"

"Casualties minimal. Terran fleet can be avoided, disabled."

"Like you disabled the *Bismarck*?"

"More energy efficient procedures, approaches, methods. Network infiltration, infection, disruption allows software disabling, paralysis, delay."

"I know this is a long shot, but... what if Sol is attacked at the same time? Can you 'un-disable' the Terran ships quickly if they have to fight?"

"Likely. Counter-proposal: Sol defended, protected, guarded by Shiny fleet."

"Ah, yes, I guess that makes sense. How many ships do you have?"

"Seven."

"Wow. Okay. Be careful, Shiny. Each Space Force man and woman that gets killed is less chance for an optimal outcome. Your return on this goes down, you understand?"

"Affirmative."

"The PIT team needs to get several places in the system. Can you hide our transports?"

"Affirmative."

"And you can use Jason's network to do all the scans our team needs to do to determine who is Trilisk and who isn't? We want to be sure. I don't want to kill any people I'm not sure about."

Yet I'm not naive enough to think this can happen without death. Someone, somewhere, is going to die. And it will be on me.

"Affirmative."

"You have the satellites ready to deploy that will hit them?"

"Affirmative."

"So this will be a piece of cake."

"Likely, probable, sure."

Telisa relaxed a bit.

Kirizzo is confident. If things get dicey, we could always use the AI.

Michael McCloskey

Chapter 8

I can't believe I'm finally a real member of the PIT team, Jason thought. He had just finished a round of virtual training with Telisa, Caden, Imanol, and Siobhan. They chatted in person, talking about their performance. In Jason's case, the chat was mostly about his mistakes, but he did not let that get him down.

Every member of the team was driven to accomplish great things, though they were not always perfectly in line with what Telisa wanted. Jason felt that Cilreth and Maxsym seemed absorbed in their own pursuits and stood apart from the others, who trained together every day in simulated battles. Jason had joined those ranks, and in the last week he had died a hundred different ways in VR training.

Jason sucked with most hand-held weapons. He knew it. The only area he could hold his own was with a rifle. He had taken up shooting after joining PIT. It was his way of pretending that he had a skill they could ever use in the field. That head start served him well now. Caden and Telisa out-shot him, but he felt he was better at hitting a target than the others when his nerves were not frazzled. He knew how to set up targeting software and configure his rounds for a dozen different long range projectile weapons. He had even practiced plain old manual sighting with three different weapons, just in case he ever had to use a weapon with dead or disabled software.

Jason had accidentally cut off his own leg with a Veer Ultrasharp three times in simulations. The swords were so sharp even their scabbards had to lock onto the handle, because almost nothing could safely hold the blade unless it clamped onto the sides. Telisa had told him it did not matter much, since they were mostly about advanced ranged weapons, but he kept trying. The sword combat interested him, but he had no background in it.

Everyone thinks I should be able to use a katana just because I have Asian blood, like it's something in my genes.

Telisa sent him a message asking for him to show up for a planning session on their Sol incursion. As the message came in the others paused too, so he got the feeling everyone would be there. Jason had enough time to stop by his quarters if he wanted, but there was nothing to bring. The exercise had been pure virtual so far today, so he did not have to shower or change. He just walked toward the meeting.

The *Clacker* was an amazing ship. It felt like a big building on a planet. And the technology was even better. Cilreth told him the entire ship had been Terranized in a few days. Before that it had been a collection of caves with blinking lights and moving sand.

Crazy. This huge thing is really an alien ship, but now it looks like a luxury home for humans. And we each have our own section the size of a neighborhood.

Jason was one of the first to arrive for the face to face.
Normal for the new guy, I bet.

With a jolt he realized the alien might show up. He became nervous. One by one, the others arrived, but Shiny did not come. Once everyone except Shiny had arrived, Telisa started. Her audience sat around on chairs, soft spheres, or just leaned against the rail next to a set of stairs leading out of the room.

"It's time we nail down everyone's mission so we can make more detailed plans," Telisa said. "I'll start with Siobhan because she's a bit ahead of the rest of us, I think." To Siobhan she said, "Go."

"I'm going after Kagan Spero," said Siobhan. "He's the leader of SSFC. I think he's a Trilisk. The family history is a bit vague in spots, but I see a thread of corporate leaders going way back that makes me think one Trilisk lives and takes on different identities in a fake family. Also he's very reclusive and lives on an island fortress. It all fits."

"And your plan to take on a fortress?" asked Caden.

"I have the blueprints of the complex. I know what to expect in general. Shiny is going to set me up with some high tech. My plan is not to break in and kill him, but to make him think a major assault is underway and flush him out. He has to have an evacuation plan. Once he tries to leave, by air or water, we'll have some toys surrounding the island that should get a clear shot. If I have to use the orbital network, I have that option too."

"Orbital network?" asked Imanol.

"That's my part," Jason said. He felt nervous, making him speak a bit too quickly. "I've contracted to set up a network of sensors that Shiny designed. He says he can use them to identify Trilisks for us anywhere on the surface. Then, when our Vovokan ships arrive, they'll deploy orbital assets that can strike down Trilisks we identify. We'll use this to hit some targets outright, but mostly it's a fallback in case some of our targets get away. We're lucky so many of them are on Skyhold, I think. Only a few should slip through the cracks."

"None are going to slip through the cracks," Telisa said.

I stand corrected, Jason thought.

"So ideally we would strike all of them simultaneously using this system," Caden said. "The Trilisks will warn each other if we don't strike all at once."

"You said ideally, and that pretty much is the key word," Cilreth said. Jason got the idea maybe it was the Cilreth copy. "But we have Trilisks in Space Force Command, inside fortresses, and a handful of other places. Yes, we'll strike those in the open and at the same time, when we can. Those of you going into protected places will get a head start. But after that I expect parts of the plan to drag. We'll be by the seat of our pants after that."

53

Telisa turned to Imanol.

"I need Imanol on a remote island that's home to two people on our list. This couple is immensely powerful and it's very suspicious that they're tucked away in such a faraway place. True, sometimes the rich just make beautiful palaces all over the world, but they seldom stay in just one all year long like these two. This mission could be a cakewalk, or you could be walking in to confront two powerful Trilisks. I have a feeling in my gut about these two, Imanol. I think they're Trilisks. You'll have the orbital network to support you."

"I assume it's some kind of heavily secured complex like Siobhan's?" Imanol asked.

"It appears to be a normal mansion. Large, but not a fortress at all. Of course, looks can be deceiving, especially where advanced technology is involved. We'll do some more research."

Imanol nodded.

"Caden, as I mentioned, is assigned the Trilisks in Space Force Command. Attempt to identify the targets as Terran or Trilisk. Try to take them out if they are Trilisk. If you can't take them out, try and alert the Space Force to their presence. I know all that's a tall order, Caden, especially right there in Space Force Command, but we have to try."

Caden nodded. "I know my way around the place, I think. But to get in, I would have to be Space Force."

"You are now Space Force, as far as anyone knows," Telisa said. "Shiny hacked you an identity and a high rank. We need to disguise you to look older. You look like you're fifteen," Telisa smiled for the first time that Jason had seen since the last mission.

Caden looked impressed. Telisa must have sent him more information.

"Colonel! That's wild. No one will recognize me, though."

"You're from the frontier, as far as anyone's concerned. Just back from a suppression mission and newly promoted. It will be enough to explain away any non-familiarity in the region. Of course the Space Force is too large for everyone to expect to recognize you, especially given the recent build-up."

Telisa decided to go next.

"I already told you we see most of the people on the list are at Skyhold," Telisa said. "So that's my problem. Of course at the top of my list is finding out if they are all Trilisks or what. Most likely I expect to find all those on the list are Trilisk, and a bunch of servants that aren't. If I can identify vulnerable innocents and protect them, then I can take out the Trilisks en masse."

"Protect the innocents? Could you really just evacuate them while the Trilisks stand by?" asked Siobhan.

"Maxsym is participating indirectly," Telisa said. "He's developed an agent which can be used to neutralize Trilisk hosts. *Terran* Trilisk hosts, I mean."

Everyone perked up at that one. Telisa continued.

"We'll use it on Skyhold."

"And what about... the other people?" Caden asked. "Is the poison deadly to normal Terrans?"

Telisa nodded.

"Less deadly, for what that's worth. I'm going to go there and try and get them off Skyhold. Or failing that, try and get the vulnerable ones, those very old or very young, into some shuttles or someplace I can isolate their air supply."

"That'll alert the Trilisks," Siobhan said.

"I'll set the trap first. Then I'll start getting normal people out of there."

"Maxsym has contributed greatly to my mission on Skyhold. He will stay here and continue to build up what we know about alien biology and set up a program in PIT I

55

intend to expand: analysis of alien biology and its applications to improve ourselves."

Telisa makes it sound like he'll be the director of an entire division someday, Jason thought.

"Cilreth remains in command of *Clacker*, to coordinate for all of us," Telisa said. "She'll be especially focused on the orbital assets which back up Jason's network for striking down Trilisks anywhere on Earth we find them. This network will also destroy Skyhold, and everyone on it, if that's what it comes to. I'm calling it right now. If the gas plan fails and we have to kill innocent people to kill 80 some Trilisks, we will. It's on me."

No one spoke up. Telisa continued.

"We'll keep working through details in the next couple of days. Then we'll be there. Any questions?"

Cilreth spoke quietly. "What happened to the idea that not all Trilisks might be, I don't want to say evil... that not all Trilisks might be our enemies?"

"These Trilisks could be living all over the globe, making Terran lives better. Instead I believe they're sitting at the top one hundred people of a tyrannical government. They're behind this gigantic military build up. I was being naive before. They're not our friends."

After a moment, Telisa continued.

"It was too easy to think of a super advanced race as being peaceful and wise and benevolent. That was a false vision all along I put into my head. I invented them before I had really learned about them. I had preconceived notions. Romanticized notions. Now, it's time to save Earth."

It was hard for Telisa to see that. She's come a long way, Jason thought.

Everyone mulled it over.

"Send me the questions as they occur to you. Poke holes in the plans all you want and let me know. If we have to make modifications I want to know sooner rather than later."

Michael McCloskey

Chapter 9

Telisa prepared to communicate with the ships she had detained in deep space. She thought about how angry they must be at her. Right now, they were sure she was the enemy. The thoughts reminded her of the prisoner she had been keeping: Krellis.

"Cilreth, I need a standard Terran space shuttle," she sent to her friend. "Just an average shuttle. We need to put the prisoner Krellis onto it and send it over to the *Bismarck*."

"Sure thing," Cilreth2 answered. Apparently Cilreth's double had access to link messages to Cilreth. "I'll ask Shiny to pray one up for us. Or do you need me to synthesize one myself?"

"Fastest way possible. Have some soldier bots escort Krellis onto the shuttle once it's ready, please."

"Got it covered," Cilreth2 said.

Telisa got a link to Admiral Sager on the *Bismarck*. This time, she did not bother with a visual feed.

"We're outside the Sol system and about to begin. I'm sure you hate us very much. Yet I hope you've at least thought about what you're going to do when we release you. Some of the most powerful and influential members of society will be gone."

"I actually wish you were from the UED," Sager said. "Never thought I'd say that to someone, but at least they would be human."

"I *am* human, but I know what you mean," Telisa said. "You'll have to declare martial law, I think," Telisa said.

"My authority would not extend that far," Sager said.

"With these powerful men and women gone, an admiral—especially when acting captain of a powerful warship—will have as good a say as anyone else."

"Can I speak with your father? Is he with you?"

"He died out past the frontier." Telisa took a deep breath. "We lost several people out there. By the way, I have a Space Force man to return to you. He was sent to spy on us. I'll be sending him on a shuttle."

"We refuse to accept any boarders until we are released," Sager said.

"Then I hope he has enough air until we leave," Telisa said. She cut the connection. Right now, what was important was cleaning up the Trilisks. Nothing she could say would be received well by the Space Force ship. They probably suspected her to be a fake personality created by the aliens that had captured them. The twist of her relationship to Captain Relachik must be odd to them— wouldn't it be more likely for the aliens to have captured Relachik and drawn her from his memory? Yet Relachik was no longer commanding the *Seeker* when it was destroyed. They must be wondering if he was a traitor too, or even an alien android posing as a Terran.

This is not my main problem.

"We're ready Shiny," Telisa said.

"Proceeding," Shiny responded.

Most of the fleet commenced its last approach on Sol. One of Shiny's ships stayed behind to quarantine the *Bismarck* until it was time to release her.

Telisa watched in her personal view. The rest of the team must have been watching, too. They gathered at a common mess on the ship. Caden wore a Space Force field uniform, basically a minimal set of rank insignia over a Veer suit. Siobhan had a stealth suit on. Imanol carried a rifle as well as his usual collection of pistols and wore a Veer suit himself. Maxsym did not show, but Cilreth arrived to see everyone off. Telisa surveyed the PIT team. They looked nervous. She did not feel it. She was calm.

I should be nervous. I guess I just don't care as much now that I'm alone.

The *Clacker* and the other ships neared the belt.
Clacker was supposed to go very close to Earth, but the
Thumper would be staying back at the asteroid belt,
because Shiny wanted to keep the Trilisk AI as far from
Trilisks as he could. The Space Force presence did not
react to the incursion.

*The Vovokan technology is still able to hide us. For
now.*

The plan called for Shiny to reveal his ships a bit after
the teams went into action. Mass confusion would be
good, but only after everyone was in place. Alerting
everyone too soon might tighten security or give the
Trilisks time to act.

"Shiny? How is it going with the Space Force?" asked
Telisa. Her PV had the data, but so much was happening at
once that she wanted his take on it.

"Suppressing detection successfully, effectively,
efficiently," Shiny said.

The Vovokan ships scattered across the solar system.
The *Clacker* proceeded smoothly toward Earth. It was the
most carefully cloaked of all the ships. If the PIT team had
their way, no one would know it was ever there.

"Shiny offer, provide, furnish plan enhancement,"
Shiny said. Telisa could see he transmitted the message to
everyone.

"What?" Telisa asked. "Oh, you have some ideas for
the attack? It's a bit late for us to change our plans now.
We've allocated everyone, and gone through simulations
to prepare."

"Fallback, backup, plan B."

"Good. How would you capture or kill the Trilisks in
your plan B?"

"Traps prepared. Trilisk columns moved close to
Earth. Upon use, hidden bomb detonates."

"Wow! An exploding Trilisk Motel," Cilreth said.
"They would not see it?"

"Unknown. Destroy tubes with short, minimal, tiny delay," Shiny said.

"Good. If any Trilisks get through the cracks, they might end up in one of those," Imanol said. "It doesn't interfere with our plans."

Caden walked up toward Telisa and Cilreth2.

"I hate to mention this but…" Caden trailed off. He looked at Cilreth2.

"I'm headed for a Vovokan shuttle," Cilreth2 said. "Only because *Clacker* will be one of the ships closest to Earth. I'm going to rendezvous with one of Shiny's ships much farther out."

That seemed to satisfy Caden. Telisa listened but did not comment.

"Are you ready?" Telisa asked Caden. "We have a shuttle we made to bring Krellis over to the *Bismarck*. They took him after all and sent the shuttle back. I'm surprised it didn't have a bomb on it. Yes, I checked."

Caden nodded. "I have everything on me."

Telisa sent him the route to the shuttle. "Good luck," she said. She offered Caden her hand, and he shook it solemnly. "Thanks for training with me. Thanks for everything." Then he left quickly.

"You really think the *wunderkind* can take out Trilisks in the middle of Space Force Command?" Imanol asked. Despite the snarky nickname, Imanol's voice did not sound as critical for once.

"Worry about your own mission," Telisa said. "You have your Vovokan shuttle picked out?"

"Yes."

"Then I wish you luck," she said.

"Thanks, but I think you're the one that has bitten off the chewiest bite. If you can't save those people, get your ass out of there. We need you around to fight another day."

"I will. Thanks."

He thinks I'm taking the hardest mission because Magnus is gone. Maybe he's right.

Imanol followed the exit route Caden had used.

Siobhan offered her hand next. Telisa shook it. "Mine's as good as dead," she said and stomped off. Telisa lifted her eyebrow.

"It was an honor to meet you," Jason said. Telisa gave his hand a perfunctory shake too, even though they both knew it was just for following the pattern everyone else had set.

"I know today you'll earn your spot as a top member of the PIT team," Telisa said. "I may not see you again. If so, just do whatever you think is right with the company."

Jason nodded, though he looked a bit overwhelmed.

"Status Shiny?" she asked.

"Terrans have detected anomalies, oddities, disturbances. Disruption minimal," Shiny said.

If I survive this, I'm going to have to ask him for the number of people we killed. If I'm lucky, maybe I'll die and won't have to ever know.

"Then I'm headed for Skyhold."

Cilreth got up next to her. She approached Telisa and hugged her. "Good luck!" she said.

Telisa pointed the way to their ships and started to walk. Jason followed.

***

Kirizzo went to a chamber deep within one of his giant ships. Three dark columns with no controls dominated the room.

A form emerged from the shadow of one of the pillars.

"Shiny! What the hell is going on?" asked Telisa3.

"Withholding data," Kirizzo said.

"How can I do this mission without knowing what's happening? Where's Magnus and the others? The habitat? Am I a copy or the original?"

Telisa3 held out her arm and flexed, trying to measure her strength.

"Parts of plan hidden, obfuscated, withheld," Kirizzo explained. "Trilisks possess, demonstrate, utilize mind reading talents. Optimal situation: information, background, details hidden, obfuscated, withheld."

"By the Five! You can't tell me because you don't want a Trilisk to read my mind and learn something that could defeat us?"

"Correct. Trust, believe, obey Shiny for mutual benefit. Telisa absorbed mission parameters?"

"Yes. I'm going into Skyhold to take down a Trilisk there. But we were far from Earth, last I remember!"

"Correct. Situation fluid, changing, shifting. Optimal course explained, given, delineated by mission briefing."

Kirizzo could tell Telisa3 had doubts. She took a long moment to look at Kirizzo. Telisa3 seemed to come to a decision after a typically short Terran planning phase.

"Okay, I'll trust you. Show me to my shuttle and I'll be off. I don't like working in the dark, but, I can see it given what you've said. If I succeed, I expect a full debriefing, in the other direction."

Kirizzo sent her a route.

"It's customary to wish me luck," Telisa3 prompted.

"Good luck," Kirizzo said. He understood that was the expected phrase the Terran had asked for.

"Say it like you normally would," Telisa3 said.

Kirizzo felt perplexed. He took a guess.

"Shiny hopes, wishes, bestows luck upon Telisa."

"Better," she said, yet hesitated. "I have so many questions… sounds like the less I know, the better? I don't like it. You can't even tell me where the others are? Magnus?"

Kirizzo was familiar with this behavior. Called complaints, these statements were a form of soft negotiation which hinged upon the compassion of the listener. Kirizzo refused to budge.

Telisa3 slowly left the room.

Kirizzo checked Telisa3's internal bomb. Its diagnostic reported full function. Kirizzo felt satisfied. When Telisa3 came under Trilisk control, it would activate, releasing the agent that Kirizzo had copied from Maxsym's lab. Kirizzo hoped that would come as a surprise to the Trilisks.

A humming noise arose behind Kirizzo. The column released another Terran.

"Shiny? Where is everyone?" called Magnus3.

"Magnus has learned, studied, absorbed mission parameters?" Kirizzo asked.

Michael McCloskey

Chapter 10

Imanol's shuttle floated on the water beside a rocky but beautiful island in the Aegean Sea. He opened a top hatch and climbed out. The sun felt warm on his face but the wind was cool. He smelled the complexity of planetary air.

Imanol lingered only a couple of seconds, then he was back to business. He grabbed his pack and slung it over his shoulder. Then he took a large black case and tossed it into the water. It floated nearby. Imanol slid down an angled side of the shuttle and slipped in. He swam slowly away from the shuttle, pulling the case with him.

Four attendant spheres skimmed the water nearby, zipping around like nervous dragonflies. He lingered in the water, waiting for the attendants to scan for hidden sensors or traps. They did not detect any danger. It was almost time. A couple of minutes had been allocated for him to apply countermeasures to any sensors or security systems he discovered on the beach. When he got the signal from the Vovokan orbs verifying it was time, Imanol got behind the case and pushed it toward shore with powerful leg kicks.

He walked out onto the sand of the island. His Veer suit had kept him dry.

So far, so good. The other team members are in action now, too.

Imanol lugged the big black case up the beach, headed for high ground. Straight ahead he saw only a rocky hill. The few trees he saw were on flatter ground to his left.

The house is supposed to be right up there.

The beach Imanol had landed on was shielded from the house by the hill. He still felt exposed out in the open. If there was hidden security the attendants failed to detect, they would notice his arrival. Then he would be walking into a trap.

He sent one of his attendants forward to verify that the island looked like he thought it should. The sensor had found the house within a minute. It was right where his intelligence said it should be. The device scanned the dwelling and found life.

Trilisks!

The scan was positive. The device told Imanol in his PV that both the targets were on the island.

Blood and souls. It's a good sign I'm not dead already. If they were all powerful, I wouldn't have even made it this far.

Imanol increased his pace. It was hard going with the heavy case, but he had been training with PIT since he joined. He had the energy he needed and lots to spare. The tiny trail he followed led up the side of a hill overlooking the house, which was built on a lower, flatter hill by a small bay. Imanol followed the general route he had used in simulations built upon their model of the island. Though the tiny details were different, the overall terrain was as expected. Imanol saw details absent in the simulations: a scrap of fabric… a lizard… a reddish rock. He stared at the rock, wondering if it held a hidden camera… or a laser.

As he neared the top of the rise he slowed. He dropped lower and crept farther, keeping his cover. Then he dropped to the ground and opened the big case.

Inside sat two cylindrical weapons secured by formed foam in the case.

Imanol pulled the first rocket launcher out of its soft prison. His plan was to kill both of them at the same time in one shot. The explosive of the warheads was surrounded by the toxin Maxsym had manufactured. That way, they might both die so quickly that there would be no response. He slung the launcher over his shoulder.

He checked his sidearms for the tenth time, even though they were configured to notify him of any problems. They told his link all was well. Then he grabbed the second launcher and turned toward the ridge he was on. He opened the electronic sight and piped it through to his link. The augmented silhouette of the house appeared in his personal view, right through the solid rock between him and the dwelling. He could see two life forms—they looked human, though running a bit hot. That was typical of the super-bodies created by the Trilisk columns.

No sign I've alerted them. This is insane. I'm shooting two near-immortal aliens on a remote island that look just like regular humans.

He watched them. One stood at a counter, perhaps a kitchen counter. The other sat nearby. He could tell by their movements that they were talking. Chatting. They looked relaxed.

I hope they come out onto their porch for some tea. Why do I feel like such a murderer? I'm doing this for all of Terra... aren't I?

Imanol could not shake his doubts. He kept arguing with himself as he scooched up to the top of the rise just a meter before him.

What if these are good Trilisks? They're going to die without a chance. Snuffed out by me. I could be killing innocents. I'm going to rocket two unsuspecting... things.

He rallied his resolve.

There's no chance to win if they're warned. It's too dangerous. The risk is huge. It affects the whole planet. I can't play fair with the enemy. Not this enemy.

Imanol prepared the launcher to fire. Its missile was maneuverable enough to shoot over the ridge and rapidly line up on the house, so Imanol did not have to get a direct line of sight. He acquired the house and kept scanning the windows. He just wanted to catch sight of them—then he saw someone running for the house. He quickly sighted the weapon's targeting sensors onto the newcomer.

Imanol stared aghast. He froze.

It's not possible. That's me!!!

Imanol was paralyzed by confusion for another moment, then he understood.

It's a duplicate of me. From a Trilisk column.

"Damn it Telisa, you should have told me! This is idiotic!"

Imanol's duplicate ran up to the back of the house. The copy was wearing a Veer suit and carrying a weapon. Imanol watched through the weapon sensor. The others inside suddenly turned toward the back. The sitting one rose. They were alarmed. The duplicate paused, then entered the house. Imanol felt sure he had just broken in. One of the Trilisks grabbed a pistol from a drawer. Another grabbed a knife.

Trilisks fighting with pistols and knives?

The windows of the house shattered open. Half a second later, Imanol heard the retort of an explosion. But there was no smoke or fire.

"Blood and souls!" he exclaimed aloud.

Was that a grenade? Maybe just a frag grenade. Not incendiary, obviously.

His duplicate was off the scanner. Imanol sent an attendant sphere in closer.

Did they blow him up with a thought? Did he have an accident with a grenade? What the hell is going on?

Imanol felt acutely vulnerable again. He glanced around behind his position, but saw no danger. Then he flipped back to the rocket launcher view.

Inside the house, the two Trilisks were in distress. They fell to their knees.

Something has… poisoned them? Of course… Maxsym's gas!

"A gas grenade?" he wondered aloud. "Where did I go? Why did you guys leave me in the dark about this?"

It seemed ridiculous to think that Imanol's duplicate had blown himself to bits with a gas grenade. It just did not track.

Wait. Duplicates can be controlled by Trilisks! They must have taken control of him, had him blow himself up with the grenade. But they did not know it was poisoned.

The forms inside were still on the floor in the house.

"This is for me," Imanol said. The grim humor of his statement curled the ends of his lips up a fraction, despite the anger he still felt at being duplicated again without his permission.

Imanol launched his rocket just over the ridge with the launcher locked onto the house.

Fooooom... Kablam!

It slammed into the big house. Debris erupted from the open windows. Then the house started to burn. The bodies inside remained still.

"Insanity," Imanol muttered.

That was so easy. I was sure the Trilisks would just kill me in an instant. That one picked up a knife! Siobhan is breaking into a massive fortress and I get a duplicate and a Trilisk with a Ginsu.

Imanol took a deep breath. It was hard to believe all this was even happening. He had never experienced such major confusion in any of the drills. He admitted that was a shortfall of their training. They had dealt with reasonable contingencies, but never anything like this.

Suddenly Imanol had a dark thought.

An army of duplicates, sent to kill the Trilisks? What if I'm a duplicate, too? What if the others are experiencing the same thing? Are there several PIT teams out there and we don't even know it?

"Dammit why does everything always get so screwed up?"

Imanol discarded the spent missile cannister and unslung the other from his back. His forward attendant did not see any Terran shapes. It paused to observe a rodent fleeing the burning house. Imanol had half a mind to shoot the next rocket at it just in case it held a Trilisk. The attendants did not report it to him as a target.

Imanol made it down his hill and walked through some tall grasses toward the house. He saw something built of stone ahead, nestled against the softer hillside. It was an old archway with rotting doors. Beyond, Imanol saw the entrance had been blocked with a stone wall.

An old root cellar? Or an escape route.

Imanol told an attendant sphere to watch the old entrance. He moved around it toward the house. As he approached the smoldering porch, he drew his laser pistol and slung the missile launcher over his shoulder.

I can't believe they sent a duplicate without telling me. I'm not going to work with these bastards ever again. I could have killed myself. In either direction. In both directions!

He had watched the Trilisks fall. Now the whole house was burned almost to the ground. The plume of smoke rose high into the sky. He thought of the ashes of the other Imanol lying among the ruins. That had been a perfect copy of him.

If I had known my duplicate was on this mission, I could have gone in at the same time, we would have had a better chance.

An attendant sphere signaled for his attention. It was the one by the old cellar entrance. A scan showed that a tunnel extended from the entrance deep into the rocky ground.

Of course. It could not be that easy. But my mission is done, isn't it?

Imanol sighed. He knew he had to check it out.

Well, it was almost easy.

Chapter 11

Jason found himself on familiar ground once exiting the Vovokan shuttle. Flair Five walked near him, scanning the roof for danger. Jason looked back at his craft and saw only a Terran aerocab sitting on the landing platform. It fit into the rooftop scheme of New York perfectly. The building he had landed on was tall, over fifty stories, but there were taller ones nearby. In fact a spacescraper was adjacent to it.

Time to get to work.

Jason had set up a control center in the building below. It had everything he needed to coordinate with Cilreth. Soon they would be finding Trilisks for the orbital attack. Jason did not have to hack anything; he was authorized to access the building because Parker Interstellar Travels had paid to use the space. Tension built inside as he made his way down to his little control room. Flair Five did little to make him feel at ease.

Jason unlocked the door with his link and walked into the suite. Something was wrong. He looked around at the equipment. Everything looked intact, but some of his storage units had moved. A heavy duty window screen he had set up to hide everything from spying eyes had been folded and set against the wall. His link threw up feeds onto the view anchors he had set up on the walls.

Someone's been here.

Flair Five dropped from Jason's link. He turned to look at the guardian machine.

"I'm under network attack," Flair Five said out loud.

"Turn it off or lose it," a male voice told Jason.

Should I? Technically I should resist as much as possible...

A shot rang out. Flair Five convulsed and went still.

Why do I bother having a guard robot, anyways?

"I see your stunner. Don't reach for it," the voice said. Then a hand fished the stunner out of his suit. Jason stood still. A firm hand turned him around. Four men dressed in black had come into the room behind him. He heard more coming out of hiding in the suite.

"Jason Yang, of Parker Interstellar Travels," one of the men said. The speaker was tall, like most of the other men, fit, with short cropped hair. He had a lined face that spoke of experience.

Men in black suits. How cliche. I'm screwed.

"Yes," he said, resigned. Of course they already knew exactly who he was.

"We know what you're doing. We just want to know why," said the man. "Come with us."

Wow. That was nice. This must be the good security agency executive. Next is the bad one?

They walked over to a suite across from his own. Jason wondered what he'd done wrong. They had found him. If a Trilisk escaped because of his failure…

I waited so long to really join the PIT team. Now I failed them.

The other suite had a command center of its own. Probably set up to monitor Jason and the PIT team. The man indicated a chair in a way that did not invite refusal. Jason sat down. He received a truth check request.

Truth check. Damn. What should I do? Just say nothing.

"You know the drill, Jason. An easy way, and a hard way," the man in the black suit said.

Jason just sat there.

"Okay," the man said. He looked at another agent and pointed at Jason Yang. They closed the suite door. Jason counted his enemies. Four men and three women.

"She's going to attach a medical monitor," the agent said.

One of the women came up and put a patch on his neck. Jason glanced at her. She was a black haired beauty. He smelled her perfume. Strangely intriguing.

"Now what are you doing here, Jason?" she asked.

"I'm coordinating my sensor network to target Trilisks," Jason said.

Dammit! What the hell was that?

The male agent smiled. "See? It's always better to cooperate," he said. "Why do you think there are Trilisks out there?"

Jason did not answer.

"How do you know there's Trilisks out there?" the woman asked.

"Magnus and Telisa found out about them. Telisa talked to one," Jason said. "Why do I answer everything she asks?"

The man shrugged. "Drugs? Instinctual desire to please a pretty woman? Link programs? All of the above?"

"Dammit!" Jason said. He tried to steel himself.

"What are you going to do once you find those Trilisks, Jason?" the beautiful agent asked.

"Kill them."

"How, Jason?"

"Very soon there will be alien strike satellites above Earth. Sent by another alien we call Shiny. I'm going to help target any Trilisks that try to escape the PIT team. Or any new ones that show up."

"I take it the Trilisks figured out how to look just like us," the woman said.

"Yes. They live in human bodies. Human, but better. Stronger, faster, even immortal."

The agent traded looks with the man who had started the interrogation.

"I'm Agent Corbin. This is Agent Jones. Core World Security."

"You have to believe me," Jason said. "Earth is under alien control. We're just here to stop them. Then we leave. Just let me do my job." Jason knew they would never let him continue, but he had to try.

Do I have any evidence?

"We believe you," Corbin said.

"What? Really? That's great!"

"We're going to help you coordinate the strike grid," he said. Jason's link access returned.

What is he doing? Pretending to be convinced? What can he gain? More information?

"You think I'm crazy," Jason guessed.

"You're not crazy," Corbin said. "The sensor array is real. You paid a lot of credits to communications agents to set it up."

They think I'm part of setting the scene for an alien attack.

"You know, aliens would not need the sensor array to attack Earth. It's only because what I say about the Trilisks is real," Jason said.

"We know you're telling the truth. The truth check, remember? You passed. And we know your hardware is real. True, you might be working for invaders and not even know it. But we have control of the array now. We'll see your targets and your data identifying them."

Jason nodded.

"Truth is, we've known about the influence of aliens on Earth for a while now," Corbin said. "If what you say is true, you're our best chance of getting back control."

Jason could not believe his luck. Had he really just found allies in the attack?

Or are they totally just playing me to get more information? But why? I already have some ridiculous drug or something that's making me talk like a schoolboy.

"The attack on the outer solar system is from this alien, Shiny you call him?" This time it was Corbin speaking. Jason realized Corbin kept asking first because they wanted to spare him the humiliation of being forced to answer. Jason decided not to fight this time.

"Yes. He just needs to get past the Space Force to remove the Trilisks."

"What's in it for him?"

I'm risking too much by discussing it. He's just pumping me for information. I'm betraying my friends.

"He wants to steal their technology. As advanced as he is, he's not at a godlike level like they were."

Before the man asked the next question, Jason had an idea.

"You will check out the targets we get, won't you? You won't feed it through."

"What?"

"I know you won't fire without checking out the target. But that's going to alert the Trilisks. You'll lose track of it. They outclass us in so many ways. Striking them down without warning is our only hope. But I know you will try and capture the ones we test positive."

"Convince me," Corbin said. "Why should I strike them down... how did you choose the locations of the sensors? You already have an idea of where they are?"

Who they are. If I tell him its a laundry list of Earth's most powerful...

"You are right, we won't fire blindly on Earth citizens," Corbin continued. "Even though we suspect alien influence. We'll nab them, stun them before they even know what's up. Then we can check them out."

"You're playing with fire," Jason said. "There's a reason our plan involves just instantaneously vaporizing them."

The man seemed to be genuinely listening.

Too good to be true. He's pretending to listen so he can get more from me.

"Why are you pretending to be nice to me?"

"Because I want to save the Earth."

Jason shook his head. "You have no idea how much I hope you're telling the truth."

"Let's move out. We've set up a temporary command center nearby. We can coordinate the operation from there. How much time do we have?"

I thought this suite was their command center.

"Another couple of hours," Jason said. "But I should coordinate with my friend in space before that."

"Shiny?" asked Jones.

"Cilreth," Jason said, wincing as he gave up more information. He was outclassed by these interrogators and he knew it. If only Shiny had given him means to resist. The PIT team needed something for this.

He stood Jason up and released his cuffs. Jason was still suspicious.

Don't believe anything. Question everything.

"Okay. Is it far? Which building?"

"Stark's."

"Excuse me, I thought you said—"

"Stark's," repeated Corbin. He pointed straight up for emphasis. Jason did not look up. He knew he could not see the top of the adjacent spacescraper from here.

Stark's was a dark, loud dance club that docked atop spacescrapers all around the world. The club was queen of the incarnate scene for the rich and famous. Most of the population of the core worlds had been there virtually, only a few elite had been there in person. For a fee a tourist would be allowed to inhabit the club in a virtual state though they did not exist to the people really there. At one point or another almost everyone had been a ghost in Stark's.

"Stark's is ours," Corbin said simply.

"Ridiculous!" spat Jason.

"I think what you told me was a bit more out there. Come with me," Corbin said, a hint of impatience in his voice.

"Uhm…" Jason said uncertainly.

"Yes, we'll be there incarnate," Corbin said. They walked out of the suite flanked by men and women in suits.

"Good thing I wasn't ordered to keep a low profile," Jason said.

"We won't have time to mingle. Saving the Earth, and all."

"Right. Of course."

Jones read Jason's demeanor.

"I'm sorry, Jason," she said. "I've been through it. I know it's humiliating, not being able to resist questions."

"Well of course I'm in the mood to accept your apology, given I'm not in control of myself."

"Yes. I'm apologizing anyway, for what it's worth."

"I don't care about the humiliation," Jason said. "I've let my team down."

She nodded. She looked genuinely sad, he thought.

Or is it just the drugs and the link hack?

The group got into a lift. Some of the suits remained outside. Four of them including Jones and Corbin were with Jason. The lift accelerated them sideways first, taking them into the next building. Then it whisked them up, up, up. Jason could tell they really were going to the top platform.

The lift opened. Jason saw men in red and black outfits.

Stark's security. They were rumored to be among the best private security on the planet. Jason doubted it. More likely the best security forces kept a low profile, while Stark's had everything to gain by buffing up the reputation of their security with a lot of propaganda.

The group was ushered into the club.

This is insane. Why here of all places? Maybe I've completely lapsed into unconsciousness and this is all a crazy dream.

They walked into the main entrance of the club. It looked like an upscale spaceport. Though the club did at times travel into space, it was mostly just the theme Stark's had chosen. The light dropped and the blare of music rose as they passed the first sound curtain. The previous song was just ramping down. Jason looked around. He saw two dozen rich, handsome men and even more sleek, beautiful women. His group got onto the right 'runway', a long wide conveyor of lighter colored floor with big red arrows that flashed down it, indicating the direction of travel. The runway ran around the outside perimeter of the club.

Jason heard Shiori start to scold the clientele. He searched for her in the control nest and found her. A dark Asian beauty with spiked black hair, Shiori spoke to the audience between songs. Her job in the club had bought her almost as much celebrity as the famous people who came to the club incarnate. Jason knew some Japanese, but Shiori's pointed and witty remarks were far too complex for his comprehension. And it did not matter; her voice was beautiful and it all blended into the atmosphere. She was supposed to sound like she was making announcements on the public link channel of an airport, but she was actually launching the most vile insults imaginable.

Blazing Flame Dance tore through the club, causing it to come alive around a hundred dancers.

A woman in a black dress with flickering green lightning dancing across its curvy surface approached the group.

"Dance me up?" she called, beckoning Jason. Corbin paused. Was that a slight smile on his lips?

Jason gave the woman his best smile. "Raincheck? I've got to save the Earth."

"You'd better," the woman said, and turned away.

She must have mistaken my captors for bodyguards.

Jason's group continued. They came to one of the executive room entrances on the outside of the runway. The group moved through the entrance and activated a privacy curtain behind. The sounds of the club became muted. The dark club beyond became hazy, a feedback indicator that they were no longer visible from outside.

A wall had been put up to shield the room beyond. They walked around it and Jason saw another workplace used by Core World Security.

Seeing the number of technicians and view anchors all over the room, Jason had no doubt this was the real nerve center he had mistaken the other suite to be.

Stark's has a CWS station? I never would have guessed in a million years. I suppose that's the point.

Corbin pointed at a chair. Jason sat yet again. He felt no anger at being their pawn. He wondered if the drugs still coursed through his system, robbing him of self determination.

"Okay, contact your friend. Let's get started," Corbin said.

Jason wondered if they wanted to find Cilreth.

Good luck to them if they do, he thought. *The Clacker is more than a match for them.*

He connected to Cilreth.

"Jason! I thought they got you."

"The other guys got me," Jason said. "Core World Security. But they want to work with us."

"Seriously? They believe you? I mean, that's great. Well we're gonna need their help. I'm under attack here. Cilreth2 is missing."

"Who is that?" Corbin asked out loud.

Ah of course. Corbin is in my link, hearing my convos.

81

"Her… our teammate," Jason said offline. "It could be her that's doing the attack. Trilisks have some limited mind control."

I can't tell them all this crap. Concentrate.

"Give me a location on a target. We don't have much time before it starts, from what I understand. I need to do the grab. We've got teams all over the Earth," Corbin said.

Chapter 12

Cilreth watched from her dark control pod on the *Clacker* as the Vovokan attack satellites deployed. Their sizes varied across several classes. The biggest one packed enough punch to blow through a spacescraper all the way to the basement. Others required the target to be out in the open.

Cilreth mentally danced around the dilemma that could pose. Would killing the last Trilisk on Earth and freeing all humanity be worth wasting a spacescraper full of people? How could anyone even make a decision like that?

She checked everything. She needed to notice remaining problems now. Something caught her eye. A slight anomaly on a computing resources usage display.

What is that?

Cilreth zeroed in on a modest section of the Clacker's computational power. It was less than one percent of her total, but it was working hard and she did not know what for. It was not doing anything Cilreth or the *Clacker* had told it to do.

I thought I had locked everything and everyone out. Even Shiny. Cilreth2 probably made some last minute change and didn't have time to tell me.

Cilreth asked her link if it had suppressed any messages from her double lately. There were no deferred communications.

The anomaly grew slightly. Cilreth went to work to eradicate the incongruity. She allocated ten percent of Clacker's computing power to finding the rogue elements and setting them back to known states. The problem seemed small, but Cilreth knew that did not mean much—at the speed of Vovokan computation, a small problem could become a big problem in the blink of an eye.

The oddity got squeezed away by her actions. She compartmentalized important systems and strengthened requirements for running tasks across logical boundaries in the ship. Vovokan computers had a maze of authorization types, each of which had a continuum of security levels. It all made her head hurt.

There. Cilreth felt the flush of victory. Until a moment later, when she saw it crop up again.

What's the problem Cilreth? This is a symptom. What's the source? An attack. Do Vovokan computers get sick?

"Cilreth. I need you. I need your super-help!" she sent to Cilreth2.

There was no answer. Cilreth checked Cilreth2's location. There was no report.

"What the…"

Cilreth2 was not answering… was she having trouble on one of Shiny's ships? Would the alien have locked her out of everything?

Shiny may have quarantined her as an extra safety measure.

Cilreth forced herself to think about other, even darker alternative theories.

A Trilisk could have control of her. Maybe she only pretended to leave the Clacker. Stealthed out? Or hacked out? She could be doing this.

Cilreth shook her head. "I don't know it's her. I don't know who it is," she said to herself aloud.

Jason came back online and requested a connection.

Hrm. Suspicious. Cilreth attached a security program to monitor his feeds.

"Jason! I thought they got you."

"The other guys got me," Jason said. "Core World Security. But they want to work with us."

What's wrong with this picture?

"Seriously? They believe you?" Cilreth decided to roll with it. "I mean, that's great. Well we're gonna need their help. I'm under attack here. Cilreth2 is missing."

Coincidence? Yes. No.

Cilreth grudgingly restricted Cilreth2's privileges to those of a simple guest of the ship. Then she started to eradicate the sick parts of the system again.

"They say it's a no go unless we verify one first."

"What? I'll hack it back," Cilreth said.

"No. We can risk one. They're going to have a half dozen snipers stun it simultaneously. Then they'll have some doctors check it out. If we can find one in a big city where he has a team, he says, a few minutes later, we can fire at will."

"I still say hack it," she said.

"Let's keep in mind I'm their captive…"

"That's okay. You're pretty new to the team," Cilreth said. She smiled.

"Uhm…"

"Okay, Telisa's not here so… I agree to their terms. But two minutes later and I'm going for it one way or another."

As it is, this could be a monumental screwup. We're talking about creatures that might be able to escape with milliseconds, who knows, maybe nanoseconds of warning. But the reality is our people won't be able to strike that close together despite our attempts to synchronize. They are all going to find different levels of resistance.

Each of the PIT members who went out to hunt Trilisks had timetables. Those with more to do started earlier than others. The ones who found themselves ahead of schedule would delay, and those behind would try their best to take shortcuts and catch up. Everyone knew the optimum time to strike. They also knew it was an impossible order. The strikes would not all fall at the same time.

Cilreth received another link request. It identified itself as 'Corbin', though the source block was not filled out correctly and it came from…. CWS.

"Corbin wants to come in on the channel."

He wants to hack us? He'll have to get in line. No doubt he's already listening in on Jason's end, anyway.

Cilreth double checked her security program. No signs of any problems.

Corbin could be a Trilisk, she thought. *Dammit. I'm already somehow under attack… and the deadline is approaching.*

"Okay," she said. Corbin connected. The sensor network went live.

"We have half a dozen positive scans. All over Earth," Corbin said.

At that moment, the entire scheme, based on a theory, became more real to Cilreth.

They really are here. At least there's not many on the surface.

"I'm selecting this one," Jason's voice said. "Right here in New York."

"Okay, let me know if you change your mind about the first one. I have my hands full here," Cilreth said.

"Acknowledged," Jason said.

A new sliver of Vovokan computation power remained rogue. Cilreth had stamped it out several times now, but somehow, somewhere, it kept coming back.

"What's happening?" Cilreth said to herself. She pushed down her frustration.

The only sources I can think of are: Cilreth2, Shiny, or Trilisks. Cilreth2 would have enough inside info and authorization to kick off some bug like this.

Shiny, of course, knew Vovokan tech inside and out. Trilisks, well, were Trilisks. They were capable of anything in their prime.

I can't believe this is happening. The most logical explanation is Cilreth2 because she's missing. I'm fighting my superior self. Or did someone take her out of the way so she couldn't help me? Dammit!

A new feed came in as a team moved in on a target in New York. The Trilisk was in the body of a young man in an apartment. The man did not move—he appeared to be in a VR. The team was setting up outside the apartment. So far, the target did not seem to be alerted.

Cilreth prepared her satellites to strike. With a single thought she believed she could crack the sensor network, find the targets, and attack them all simultaneously. It was still early according to the plan. The other PIT teams were just now going in.

Cilreth half watched the feed. The CWS team was ready to go in. Cilreth noted most of them were androids. They had violated old laws by making them indistinguishable from real humans, but Cilreth was not about to complain about it in the middle of the most critical moment of the attack. The team broke the security of the room, slipped in, and assaulted the Trilisk. The androids ran into the room and stunned the host. Government people flooded into the room.

They were telling the truth. They really are checking Jason's story. They must have had some pretty strong suspicions.

The word came through in less than a minute.

"Not human. Repeat, this is not human!" a voice reported. Cilreth assumed it was one of the field doctors.

"I knew I was making the right play to back you, Jason," Corbin said. "Maybe it was that honest face of yours. The sensor net is at your disposal."

"You heard that, Cilreth? We're a go," Jason said. His voice sounded anxious. Jason had agreed to have his vitals monitored for the mission. Cilreth saw he was stressed but not to the level where he was actively afraid for his life.

"Only a couple more minutes," Cilreth said. "I have the targets in my sites."

"I hope collateral damage will be minimal," Corbin said. "We're getting some scary reports about losses out in the belt."

Just the Space Force panicking, Cilreth thought. *Shiny has cut them all off from each other.*

Cilreth armed the satellites at the appointed time. Five more Trilisks were on the sensor net. The other teams had gone in a few minutes ago. It was time.

"The shots are pretty clean," she said. *If we're lucky, not a single side injury. But I won't say that unless it happens.*

Cilreth checked the numbers on the *Clacker* problem. Three percent of her resources were fighting her.

Cilreth told the satellites to fire.

Her personal view indicated the strikes went out. Two seconds later, the sensor network reported success.

"If the sensor network still works, if they haven't fooled us, we got them," Cilreth said. "We still need to back up some other targets, though. We have team members going after some others we could not scan."

"Corbin? Is the feed real?" Jason said.

"Yes. It's real. We haven't fed you a fake."

If it's not, when would Corbin come clean? Never? If it's fake, we just shot at random into several cities.

Cilreth wanted to check the integrity of the sensor network herself, but she was much more concerned about the anomaly on *Clacker*.

"Let me know if any more show up," Cilreth said. "I still have a problem here."

"Got it," Jason said.

Maybe I can eliminate one of the possible sources with a bluff.

"Shiny! Shiny, stop attacking the *Clacker*!" Cilreth sent. "I know it's you!"

There was no response.

"By Cthulhu!"

Okay… I can talk to Jason, still. Who else?

Cilreth opened her communications net wider. She picked up on a lot of traffic on the Terran network. The most interesting activity was coming from the Space Force, which of course was on high alert due to Shiny's distractions. Cilreth decided to listen in on some and see what the Space Force knew.

Cilreth's eyes grew wide. She stopped breathing for a moment. Then she just sat in shock.

"We're screwed eight ways from extinction," she muttered.

Michael McCloskey

Chapter 13

Caden stepped out of his shuttle onto a huge docking area on Space Force Command.

SFC was a huge orbital habitat above Earth. A giant gravity spinner allowed the base to stay in peaceful orbit around Sol with the home planet. Using the spinner, the habitat did not have to orbit Earth, but an asset this valuable was kept close to the heaviest defenses the Terrans had.

I know what I have to do, he told himself. His heart raced and his palms were sweaty. This was the center of the Space Force. He had dreamed about coming here so many times, under very different circumstances.

I have to calm down. I'm going to activate a hostile intention trigger walking around like this.

He took a deep breath. He had done enough VR simulations of this to take the edge off any normal nervousness, but the enormity of this task had him feeling the pressure.

Fortunately Caden was no stranger to pressure.

He slipped one of his four attendant spheres out of his pocket. He told the attendant to electronically disguise itself as a simple courier robot. Robots were commonplace here and on Earth. Each one had to obtain an ID and authorization for every task it undertook. Luckily Shiny had the edge when it came to security technology.

Find me my Trilisks, little one.

The attendant flew away eagerly. Caden looked down at himself.

I could have been in this uniform legitimately, he thought. *Though I wouldn't already be at this rank.*

Caden followed the flow of traffic from the starport hub. He felt that he blended in completely. Everyone was in a hurry. Clearly the activity in the outer system had caused a stir here. He picked up a news feed.

All personnel had been called in from all forms of leave. The Space Force was on red alert.

Everyone knows the aliens are here. They think the aliens are here to hurt them, not save them.

Caden stepped aside into a comm niche along the side of the wide corridor. He could call anyone in the system with his link, but the niche could supply a video feed for the other parties of his call, a sound curtain, and refreshments. Caden really wanted just a bit more privacy for the next step.

He sat in the niche in front of the camera and let another attendant free. It hovered in the comm niche and connected to the base directory. Caden let it do its work.

I feel like a traitor. I shouldn't be hacking Space Force security. I know I'm helping, but it feels so wrong.

The attendant managed to attain a high security clearance and retrieved the location of three admirals. The men who PIT suspected of being at high risk of Trilisk control. Caden dispatched the closest position to his attendant that had already gone ahead. It would be near the admiral within the minute.

Caden left the tiny booth. He moved faster now that he had a clear destination. He walked down a side corridor, headed to another deck above him in the gravitic orientation of the base.

All around the system, the PIT team is hunting Trilisks.

Caden stepped into a gravity free tube to be whisked upwards in a stiff stream of air. At the next level he grabbed an exit bar and swung out.

I'm close now, he thought, looking at his link map.

Caden turned another corner and got the man in sight. He checked the uniform. It indicated the man was an admiral. His lead attendant had completed its scan: The admiral was a Trilisk host body.

He must be between meetings… my time is running out.

The corridor was not empty. Besides, everyplace on the base was monitored by the security AI. Once he acted, it would not be long at all before armed robots would be moving in on him. His chances of taking out a second Trilisk would be low, but he might scare the others into running into Shiny's backup trap.

Caden told two of his attendant spheres to go find the other admirals. Each of them had small payloads of Maxsym's deadly gas. They would have a fair chance of killing the others within the next couple of minutes.

The admiral turned a corner ahead into an adjoining room. Caden followed. Other officers were coming from behind. Caden thought they might be headed for the same room. When Caden arrived at the door, he entered and activated his stealth suit.

A couple of officers behind him stopped in shock. In one more second, they would think to warn the admiral. The Trilisk admiral stood in the room, looking to one side. A hologram of the system dominated the center table. The rest of the room was filled with anchor points that looked empty to Caden but no doubt held data displays for everyone else. One other person, a female commander was in the room.

Caden drew his laser. He told it to shoot the enemy. His laser refused to fire.

Oh no…

The man's head snapped up to examine Caden. Caden did not know what had alerted the target. Somehow, the admiral seemed to lock eyes onto Caden.

Strong, fast… untrained?

Caden prepared to defend himself against a superhuman foe.

The scouting attendant came into Caden's line of sight behind the Trilisk host. It accelerated to a blur and smashed into the back of the admiral's skull. The man dropped. The sphere reported that the target was dead.

"Admiral!" someone called out. Everyone in the room ran toward their fallen admiral. Caden felt only relief.

"Intruder alert!" a broadcast announced. Everyone in the room took their attention off the admiral and started to look around. The broadcast had indicated Caden's current position exactly.

What? I've received no message, but something's obviously up! They know I'm here.

Suddenly a man appeared in the doorway with a stunner in his hand, aimed at Caden. Caden threw himself aside and fired his laser. This time the laser activated. Both weapons hit their targets. The man fell, a hole in his shoulder. Caden staggered. His suit had protected him from most of the stunner energy, but it still confused him for a moment.

In that moment, Caden became caught in two glue grenades. More men moved in.

Stealth suit fail, Caden thought. Glue covered his face. He tried to think of a way out, but he lost consciousness before succeeding.

***

Caden could smell solvent on the air. He looked down at himself. His suit had been disabled. It had several globs of glue stuck to it. His surroundings looked like a typical interrogation room. Dark gray, bland, almost empty, secure. A man confronted him. He looked angry.

I wonder if we got the others.

The interrogator spoke.

"Aliens are attacking. Now, we have three dead admirals on our hands in as many minutes. You're a part of it."

"I'm one of the good guys."

Three dead admirals! Excellent.

"Then accept our truth check mode."

Caden nodded. The man looked surprised. The truth check engaged. The inquisitor could now use Caden's own link against him.

"Tell me what this is about. Who sent you? We know you've been to the frontier."

He thinks I'm from a terrorist faction. Or taken over by alien mind control.

"Check the bodies. They're not human!" Caden said.

"Ridiculous," the man said. "My own eyes—"

"Your eyes are wrong. I scanned him before I took him down. He was an alien. Placed high to control things here."

The man obviously wanted to see that Caden was lying, but the truth check must have verified his statements.

"Any doctor can tell you in five minutes," Caden said. "Just examine them."

The man did not respond. He was busy on his link.

Lousy interrogator. I can tell all kinds of crap is going down. He's distracted.

"How did you close in on me so fast, anyway?" Caden asked.

The man smiled. "Aigis saw two of you. Clones. Pretty sloppy of you. I suppose to aliens like you, we all look alike anyway!"

Aigis was the Space Force Command security AI. Caden had read about it as a kid. It was a famous entity working for the Space Force, although not as famous as its grand strategist, Caisar.

"Clones?"

Oh crap.

"Yep. Sorry to say your copy didn't make it. But you knew that. Were you supposed to explode too? Another suicide bomber?"

"No. I don't know what you're talking about."

The man shook his head. "By the Five," he muttered. He was seeing that Caden believed his answer.

He thinks I'm a mind slave. Brainwashed and sent on a suicide attack…

"What is the toxic gas you've released?"

"I shot an alien pretending to be an admiral. If you check the body, you'll see everything's not right with it. He was stronger and faster than he should have been, and immortal besides. The gas kills them."

"Well, it's made several people very sick."

"The robots did not release enough to hurt anyone."

"It was in the bomb your double detonated. We have people in the infirmary!"

"They're young and fit? It's only truly deadly to Trilisk hosts," Caden said.

My double blew up a bomb. That won't help me.

"*Trilisk hosts?*"

"My first target was one. And if two admirals dropped like flies when that gas hit, then they were Trilisk hosts, too."

"Why did you decide to betray Earth? Why would you participate in the alien attack?"

"Please keep up? Everything's fine. We came to get rid of the Trilisks. The less you resist, the fewer men and women that will be hurt. Just let the ships come and they'll leave when the Trilisks are removed."

The man turned bright red. Caden was startled.

"The less we resist?! Thousands are dead! They didn't have a chance to fight back!" the man yelled.

"What? Thousands? You said only a few are sick from the gas."

Shit. Did the gas effect normal people, too?

"Titan. Ganymede. All three belt city Space Force bases. Destroyed!" the man said.

Caden could not speak for a moment.

What have I done? Shiny did that?

"They're not destroyed. You just can't reach them. Your communications have been scrambled," Caden said. A horrible feeling started to settle in his stomach.

It took his interrogator a moment to respond. Caden received a pointer to his link. It was a video capture.

Caden saw a Space Force base built into a large asteroid. Some kind of missile shot toward it. The base exploded. Pieces of the structure hurtled into space. Caden could hear the chatter of radio traffic in the background... filled with calls for help.

"Destroyed by... the large spherical ships?"

"I have no idea. They're gone. No one can reach Mars Defense. The attack has been moving steadily through the system. Earth is next. SFC is next."

Michael McCloskey

Chapter 14

Siobhan submerged her Vovokan shuttle in the ocean a good distance from the Spero island compound. She took a moment to gather her equipment and her thoughts for the assault.

I have to do this. I have to make this frackjammer pay for what he did to us.

Siobhan admitted to herself she cared about this revenge more than anything else. A better person would have been focused on Earth, on freeing humanity, but Siobhan knew she was not that person. The primary reason for her existence was to snuff out Spero. She accepted it.

I don't care what anyone thinks. I don't care. He will die for this. Then I'll do whatever I can to stop the other Trilisks.

As agreed, Shiny had provided her with new toys for the mission. She had a Vovokan subverter device she could use to take over Terran electronics. She did not understand its workings, but Shiny's instructions were clear and simple: scan the target's link interfaces to get a report on its weaknesses; then, one of the weaknesses could be exploited to gain control of the target.

Of course, the Terran link interfaces had been hardened by countless attacks. One by one the flaws had been discovered and shored up. New link interfaces never went into widespread use until they had been tested for years, often including close scrutiny by AI experts. Nevertheless, Shiny obviously had a few high tech tricks up his sleeve that allowed him to circumvent Terran link security. Perhaps he had uncovered UNSF back doors, or maybe he could use EM fields to change bits inside the hardware indirectly, creating an opening. In any case, Shiny's report indicated almost any Terran device would be vulnerable.

Siobhan would have been happy with that alone, but Shiny had given her two more items: a stealth suit, and a weapon.

Siobhan had been told it was based upon Cilreth's stealth suit, but Shiny had made some improvements to its power and subtlety. The Vovokan had also made some tweaks to the suit's software. She wore the suit now. It reported itself at full charge and readiness.

That left her weapon. It looked like a heavy pistol, with an additional grip under the barrel for steadying its weight. Siobhan had no idea what it fired. The link interface reported 200 bio-target shots and Shiny had told her, one shot would be fatal to any human, Trilisk-enhanced or otherwise, that wore a Veer skinsuit or less. It also reported a magazine of 50 mech-target shots, which were for robots, hardpoints, or Terrans in full combat armor. The analysis said she should be able to one-shot anything up to a tank.

The range of the weapon left her stunned. Shiny's specs reported a range of one kilometer for the bio shots, and ten kilometers for the mech shots. The weapon could not lock onto anything so far away by itself, but with the help of a simple attendant sphere, the heavy pistol could kill anything on the island from anywhere else on the island. If she was inside or her target was inside, then it became much less sure.

Her plan was to utilize this amazing weapon to its fullest. She would deploy attendants around the island as spotters for her target. Then, rather than shoot it out with Spero in his stronghold, she would spook him out. Once out of the building, the attendants could spot for her. It should only take one or two long range shots to kill him.

He would never know what hit him, and he would have no chance to shoot back.

Siobhan opened the shuttle's modest cargo bay and let the ocean come in. She stabilized herself until the water

had flowed in, then swam out. Behind
insectoid soldier robots unfolded and
would help provide the pressure to dr
fortress.

Siobhan headed toward the islan
soldiers followed her for a while, but
ten to each side, to move to other spots on the island.
Siobhan wanted it to appear like the compound was
surrounded by a small army. She figured that would
pressure Spero into running for it.

Siobhan activated her stealth suit and emerged onto a
sandy beach. Her attendants noticed a couple of electronic
monitors meant to detect trespassers. Siobhan moved
slowly by, relying upon her suit. She saw her position on
the island in her tactical. Her link showed her an optimum
path to one side of the compound.

Siobhan had purposefully selected the end of the
compound that looked the most remote. She wanted to
pressure Spero, flush him out. If possible, she would avoid
as much of the security as she could.

*The attack on the outer system should help. He knows
something is coming.*

Siobhan walked into the vegetation of the island. The
surface was rough. A few tree crabs scuttled for cover. She
had to climb down into a depression and back up again on
her way. The ferns and palms were dense, but it made her
feel safer. She watched the soldiers and attendants take
their positions with her PV.

Siobhan proceeded an eighth of a kilometer through
dense jungle, then stopped. She heard something. Then she
saw something metal through the ferns. A large machine
moved up ahead.

It had two metal legs lifting it above the foliage of the
island floor. Its gray and red metal body looked vaguely
humanoid and heavily armored. There could not have been
a person inside, as the waist was impossibly thin,

ed of only a shiny column that looked like a
ic spine. A sleek, arched chestplate opened for four
y tentacles of carbon or metal. Weapons systems built
nto arms and head were unmistakable. A pair of baneful
red eyes surveyed the jungle from its armored head.

That thing was designed to intimidate.

She checked its interfaces with the subverter.

Custom software. Source unknown.

Then the machine closed off all communications. The subverter had alarmed it.

Fsssssss.

Flame engulfed the area. Siobhan immediately felt it through her suit.

Krumpf.

Sliced fronds, branches, and sand sprayed over her from her right flank.

Can it see me?

Siobhan darted away through the burning foliage. She zigzagged back into cover, dancing around branches and leaves. She drew oxygen from the suit's supply. As the smoke cleared, she stopped again in a crouch to look back.

The green plants did not burn well. Most of the flames had died down. The machine had cleared a small area of plant matter. The sandy soil exposed was blackened and littered with jungle debris.

Siobhan caught sight of the machine again. It had lifted two meters off the ground, leaving its legs dangling in midair. It did not seem to be looking at her. A laser probe flashed from its head, checking for hidden objects. The machine patrolled about in the air, searching for her.

No hacking this one, Siobhan thought. *Run or fight.*

Siobhan brought up her weapon and loosed two mech rounds.

Blam! Blam!

Bright flashes popped among the bright green fronds between her and the robot. Something had stopped the rounds. The machine started to scan in her direction. She turned and ran.

So much for Shiny's fancy gun! Damn it! How could this machine be so powerful? I wonder if the suit's sound curtain could cover such loud sounds.

The machine came after her. She could see it in the view of a couple of her attendants nearby. She ran as fast as she could through the jungle without regard for direction.

It's not supposed to be able to see me. Did Shiny betray me?

Siobhan looked back. She had broken some fronds in her hasty passage. Did the machine see that? She looked at the ground. Just out of the range of her stealth suit, she saw one of her footprints deep in the crushed leaves covering the sandy ground.

I'm helping it by leaving footprints behind.

Siobhan jumped onto a rock, took three steps and then scrambled up a tree with thick, soft branches. She slowed. The huge green fronds hid her well, but she did not want to give away her position by moving any of them.

She heard a humming noise as the machine neared her hiding spot.

Siobhan prepared herself for another shot.

Maybe the mech round will work at point blank range.

Siobhan did not move her hand yet to aim. She just froze. She glimpsed its leg through the leaves as it hovered nearby.

The awful machine moved on.

Siobhan regained her wits. She had been nothing but a mouse running from a robotic cat there for a minute. Now, it was time to think again.

Spero had not doubt taken notice by now that something was afoot out in his vast front yard. Unless the guard machine was too dumb to report a battle with something it could not see.

That could be fine. He's alerted. He does not know how many enemies he has out here. I need to change alerted to alarmed.

Something in surveillance feed caught her eye.

Someone else is out there. They don't look like they belong.

Siobhan watched the stranger. The feed zoomed in.

Frackjammers!

The stranger looked just like her. It *was* her. As she watched, the other Siobhan leaped over a huge rock formation and landed on the other side.

Yep. A Trilisk duplicate!

"I'm going to kill somebody for copying me without my permission..."

Siobhan had the awful realization that her copy would be vulnerable to manipulation by the Trilisk. Then she would be facing the Trilisk and herself. A super-fast version of herself.

What if the Trilisk made a copy? Just to screw with me? How could it happen? Did my copy survive way back on the Blackvine habitat?

Chapter 15

Telisa's robotic carrier approached the huge mass of Skyhold. The carrier looked exactly like supply ships that came into Skyhold regularly. Only two decks and a few isolated cabins on board were pressurized. Telisa waited patiently with her cloaking device activated. With luck, she would be able to sneak on board when it was unloaded. Telisa isolated her link to help stay hidden.

The ship received a broadcast from the habitat. The message came through the public broadcast on the ship, through speakers and the link network.

"Andralede… we see you are with crew. Prepare to be boarded."

We see you are with crew? I don't think so. If they do see me, this is going to be a lot harder than I expected.

Telisa stayed put. She had her Veer suit's vacuum cover ready. If she had to move through vacuum to get inside Skyhold, she would. She had left her beloved double-triggered "lightning gun" behind. It was too heavy and probably not safe to fire on Skyhold anyway. But she missed its heft and reassurance at her back. In its place was a heavy tube filled with Maxsym's deadly compound.

The carrier attached gently to Skyhold. Telisa saw there were two connections, one on her deck and another one deck below. She moved in that direction, ready to try and slip by. When she neared the lock corridor, she took a peek. Her new eye helped her see all the way down the long corridor and took a snapshot in several wavelengths.

She saw a team moving onto the carrier from the lock corridor. They had laser carbines in their hands. Telisa was unfamiliar with their armor—it wasn't Momma Veer.

They do suspect something. Or could they really take this precaution with every ship?

Telisa found a spot to wait for them to pass. It was a rectangular maintenance access port, shoulder-width and twice as tall as a human. She slid inside.

No room to maneuver, but this is the best way to give them the slip.

The group moved by her niche silently. She felt something was wrong with them. She looked at the nearest face. It was hidden behind a smooth reflective oval mask. A green circle was emblazoned on its shoulder, the universal symbol for a robotic construct.

Androids.

As they moved away she took the corridor they had used to arrive. Since her cloaking device provided a special sound curtain as well, she decided to run for it.

I really don't want to end up having to crawl around outside the station figuring out how to get in.

She made it to the lock. The umbilical corridors remained attached and empty, though two androids stood ramrod straight at the entrance ahead.

More of them? I guess the Trilisks are serious about security. That shouldn't be surprising.

She looked at them. It was hard to force herself to walk through. She felt like they must see or hear her. The two silent humanoid shapes creeped her out.

Telisa steeled herself and kept coming. She walked right between them and stepped through the lock. She expected to see an amazing space habitat on the other side. A luxurious playground. What she saw instead gave her pause.

A huge hardpoint had been built watching the lock. More androids stood at the wall. Three laser turrets were built into the wall facing the entrance. They looked like armored pillboxes with stubby metal barrels sticking out.

Wow. Paranoid. Today, with good cause. They're going down.

Skyhold had more security than she had ever seen. Up ahead, two corridors led in and out of the station. Banks of scanners were emplaced on either side.

Telisa slipped to one side to observe. Once again she felt doubt. Was her cloaking device up to this?

The longer I stand here, the bigger the chance it runs out of juice and I'm dead.

Telisa looked at the corridors and tried to decide if she should run or walk through. She stepped on a conveyor platform that would carry her through. The conveyor whisked her past the checkpoint. Telisa caught herself holding her breath.

Crazy.

She willed the alarms to remain silent, then winced when the panel she rode on turned red. Androids started to move ahead and behind her, running along the sides of the checkpoint.

Telisa had a split second decision: freeze or run?

They see me here. The strongpoint has the most sensitive equipment. They wouldn't be able to see me inside.

She started to run forward.

I wonder what tipped them off... there must be a lot of sensors. Probably my weight on the conveyor. Maybe even the air I'm breathing. They could have chemical sniffers.

Telisa told her Veer suit to seal up. Her emergency pressure mask flipped over her head and sealed. The soft face covering hardened into a clear, optically perfect visor.

I should have done that before. I've never had the cloaking device fail though.

A squad of androids appeared at the end of the long runway she was on. They did not see her, though they held their weapons up. They started to run toward her.

Telisa hopped up on the guardrail and kept running ahead.

Nothing here, androids. Just a malfunctioning sensor in your conveyor.

None of the weapons of the androids tracked her as she ran by on the rail. Telisa did fine with her balancing act until she neared the end. Her stride got a bit of side-to-side wobble, almost sending her back onto the conveyor. Telisa accelerated, going for an all or nothing finish. More androids waited motionlessly at the end.

Telisa leaped right over them from the end of the guardrail. Her landing was rough. She faltered and had to roll straight ahead. The stealth sphere covered the noise of her impact and roll. Then she regained her feet and kept running. She soon lost herself in the wide concourses of the interior of Skyhold.

Finally on board. A bit behind schedule. The others must be well underway.

Beyond the huge strongpoint, Skyhold was every bit as luxurious as she had expected. The inside was huge, filled with gardens and tennis courts, swimming pools and zero-grav play zones. A few people walked about, though it was mostly empty. She checked the directory.

Shopping malls. How quaint. You get to go pick up the merchandise yourself instead of have it delivered. Fun for a vacation, sure, but it gets tiring fast.

Telisa did a quick Trilisk host check for everyone within range. She got no hits for about twenty people near her.

Negative. Hrm. So much for just opening the gas cannister and being done with it.

Telisa let one of her attendants hack the network around her and authorize itself as a registered courier. Then she let the attendant exit her stealth zone. It flew off to look for Trilisks. She saw a VR lounge nearby and decided to check it out.

Maybe Siobhan was wrong. Maybe the rich and powerful only need these android servants. If there are no young or old ones, I could risk the gas. Depending on how many Trilisks I find.

She looked around at the five people in the VR lounge. They looked disheveled. Unhealthy. A man sat with his arms limp at his sides and a blank look on his face, but Telisa was not sure he was even hooked up to a virtual environment. A woman sat ten meters away who looked like a drug addict. She had hollow cheeks and messy hair.

These are the rich and powerful? They look more like the inhabitants of an ancient mental health hospital.

Telisa went to the next large entertainment center, a combination restaurant and observation lounge looking out over Earth. Most of the public places on Skyhold involved either eating or exercise, since modern core worlders spent a lot of their time in virtual realities. Their real bodies still had needs, though, so the habitat provided pleasant places to feed and stay fit.

The restaurant was largely empty. That did not surprise Telisa. The rich and powerful would not enjoy struggling with crowds. The population density here was low, or at least the station was designed to make it feel that way. She saw a few couples. Her link cache told her one of them was on the list: Theo Soros. The attendants told her none of them were Trilisk. Nor was her remote attendant finding any Trilisks.

I wonder what the others are finding. Could the Trilisks have found ways to hide themselves better? Maybe the attendants just can't tell. What a disaster.

Telisa decided to take a risk. She ducked into a restroom to flip off her stealth device. She appeared in the mirror.

A bit martial looking. But if I don't take risks, I'm not going to get to the bottom of this.

She walked out into the restaurant. It felt dangerous to be out in the open, but she hoped she would have some time. She went back to the table with Mr. Soros and the woman he dined with. She sat down at the table uninvited.

"How are you two doing?" Telisa asked. "I'm with the Space Force."

The couple exchanged looks. Telisa winced internally. How would they react?

"We're getting by, considering," Mr. Soros said. Telisa detected no hint of sarcasm.

"Considering what?"

"Considering how sick I am of this place," he said. He looked at Telisa pointedly.

"Well, if you hate it so much here why don't you just leave? You must have another house somewhere," Telisa said.

Everyone here can afford several houses all over Earth.

"Yeah, why don't you fly my shuttle?" he replied harshly.

Hrm. What's that about?

"I can fly," Telisa said idly.

Mr. Soros turned to the woman across from them.

"I guess we're starting to lose it here, huh? Some of us more than others," he said sadly, tilting his head toward Telisa.

"When did they send you here?" asked the woman. She was looking at Telisa.

"Send me here? Who?"

"The Space Force? Hell I don't know *who* any more than anyone else," the woman said testily. "Whoever it is that has us all canned up here. How long ago?"

"I just got here," Telisa said.

"So you're here to make fun of the prisoners? Or did you screw up and they sent you here to rot?"

Aha.

"Oh," Telisa said, looking concerned. "Those androids are your keepers?"

"If you really don't know, then they're your keepers now too now, miss," Mr. Soros said.

Telisa's roving attendant detected androids on the way. Most likely her presence had been noticed. She wondered if the monitoring was simple or as elaborate as an AI wired into the whole network.

"I'm here to help you," Telisa said quickly. "Spread the word quietly. Help is here."

Telisa flipped on her stealth sphere.

The woman gasped. Mr. Soros stood up and looked around.

Three androids arrived as Telisa padded over to the other side of the room. She stood behind a bank of plants, even though she was invisible.

"Citizen Soros, please point out the female you were speaking with," one android said.

"Uhm… sorry. That was just a hologram," he stumbled.

"I see, Citizen Soros… please stand by." The androids stood quietly for a second. "Carry on," the android said. Then all three began to walk in different directions, scanning the room.

Hrm. I wonder if they called up to an AI. I should leave. Of course, that is what an AI would expect. I could stay.

Telisa decided to be unpredictable. Her attendant still searched around the habitat. It was looking like there were no Trilisks in Skyhold at all. Just prisoners… rich, powerful people who had been herded here and trapped.

So we had it backwards. The Trilisks decided to give themselves free roam of the system and bottled up everyone one else here.

Telisa suddenly realized she was going to have more trouble *leaving* than she had getting in. Now she was a prisoner too, with Earth's once-most-powerful.

So the other PIT team members are facing the Trilisks and I'm stuck here.

The androids searched for a minute longer, then dispersed. Telisa stayed put. She had thinking to do, anyway. An attendant brought an anomaly to her attention. It had found another attendant device that Telisa had not launched.

What is a rogue attendant doing here? No way.

Telisa got up to leave. One last thought stilled her.

Is that a clever trick? Maybe the attendant was noted, a copy was made, and... wait. I could tell if it's a copy.

Telisa told her attendant to communicate with the other one. If it knew the Vovokan protocols, it was real. Otherwise, it was part of a trap.

The other attendant responded properly. It was real, but it refused to reveal information about the owner. Telisa left the restaurant. She wanted to check this out in person.

The owner of the other one may well show up there, too.

Telisa moved quickly to the spot on the map. She had to go down two long corridors and take a grav-free tube. When she arrived, she found the two attendants staring each other down in front of another Telisa.

"The Five hate me," she said. She uncloaked herself. Telisa3 did a double take.

"Shiny didn't tell me anything," Telisa3 said. "You?"

"Shiny talked to you? Sent you? Damn him."

"Are you the original? I don't know much because the Trilisks can read minds," Telisa3 said. "I'm just supposed to find Trilisks."

"Actually I am too," Telisa said. "But there aren't any here. This place is a giant prison for the rich and powerful. I'm starting to think the Trilisks shuffled them all here so a small number of Trilisks could control them."

"So the Trilisks really are... enemies?"

"At least some of them. Maybe all."

"Your eye?"

"Battle injury," Telisa said. "This new one is fine."

"You must be a little different than me. I'm not sure I would keep the scar," Telisa3 said.

I kept it to remember.

"I'll get rid of the scar soon," Telisa lied. "If I live through this."

"Did Shiny have your permission to make me? I know I'm one of the Trilisk copies. I'm strong."

By the Five.

"What's the last thing you remember?" Telisa asked.

"We were getting ready to go after the Trilisk. On *Clacker*. We had just found a space habitat."

"The Five curse me!" Telisa spat.

"What?" Telisa3 asked.

Telisa took a deep breath.

My first instinct is to tell myself everything. Are there negative repercussions to doing that?

"Great. Just great. I'm standing here thinking about lying to myself," Telisa3 said.

"Well you trust me," Telisa said. "I'm just thinking it through a second."

Telisa3 nodded.

"You're super strong and fast," Telisa said. "You're also helpless around Trilisks. They put in a back door. A Trilisk column clone is super easy for them to mind control. About instantly."

Telisa3's mouth dropped open.

"I know," Telisa said. "We know now, Trilisks are here in the Sol System. I came to kill some in Skyhold. I don't know why Shiny would send you. Just to back me up? I guess he decided… I don't know what he was thinking! You're great for any mission but this… against anything but Trilisks! If there had been Trilisks here it would have been disastrous! They would take you over and you would help them hunt me down. It's almost like he *wants* us to fail."

"He could be Trilisk himself?" Telisa3 asked.

"Maybe. At this point I'm scared of what I don't know. But he could have just killed the whole PIT team outright. I just can't put it together."

"I don't have a cannister like that," Telisa3 said. She indicated Telisa's gas tube.

"This liquid disperses into a gas that kills Trilisk hosts quickly," Telisa said. "I brought it in case there were a lot of them here."

Telisa3 shook her head. "Why wouldn't he give some to me?"

"The Five curse me," Telisa said again, shaking her head.

"Is Magnus nearby?"

Telisa controlled herself. Barely.

"He's on another mission," she managed to say. "We need to check the rest of the base, and if there aren't any Trilisks at all, we need to leave. Somehow."

Telisa3 nodded. "Should be easy enough, with two of us. I have a stealth suit. I suppose you have the cloaking sphere?"

"Yes. But they detected me at the entrance gate."

"Really? Me, too, but I figured it was just that this suit stealth system was inferior."

"They may have detected my weight on the conveyor, or maybe smelled me with chemical sniffers," Telisa said.

"We can target the sensors," Telisa3 said. "Sniffers aren't good enough to target shots, usually," she added.

"You keep saying everything I'm thinking."

"Well duh."

They exchanged smiles. Until Telisa thought of Magnus.

I wish he was here so much.

Telisa3 misunderstood her look. "Right, back to business. We should get these people out of here. If there's a Trilisk we missed, that should get its attention."

I've changed.

Telisa nodded. "Okay. We'll pick an exit gate, preferably one with some passenger-ready ships outside. Then hit the sensors, take out the guards and get some people out."

"Attendants can find the sensors I hope," Telisa3 said.

"Hrm. Maybe another layer of disguise is in order," Telisa said thoughtfully.

Michael McCloskey

Chapter 16

As Imanol stared down the tunnel hidden inside the old root cellar, he considered simply launching a missile down the tunnel and calling it good. He knew shooting blindly was not a great strategy. He might collapse the tunnel and never find more Trilisks hiding inside. Then they could emerge a year from now and take over again.

Imanol wiped sweat from his forehead and cursed under his breath. It had been a lot of work getting through the wall built over the entrance. The root cellar was old, filled with the remains of barrels and rotting wood shelves. He hid the rocket launcher in the cellar under a rotting wooden shelf. A scenario flitted through his mind where he never came back to get the launcher and some kid found it in the cellar years after. Imanol checked the weapons lock: only the PIT team could use it.

He reviewed his weapons. Besides the laser pistol in his hand, he had a projectile pistol at his belt, a stunner in his pack, and two grenades in a special pocket of his Veer armor. He looked nervously at the tunnel entrance. It looked long unused, with roots hanging down that obscured his view.

Imanol told his laser pistol's light to activate. It complied. The light ran on the same power source as the laser, so light would not be a problem. He crouched to get a better look. The tunnel went at least twenty meters. He could not see farther than ten meters ahead.

"Are we having fun yet?" he muttered. Imanol advanced in a crouch. He sent an attendant forward to scout.

As Imanol scraped through the old tunnel, his attendant showed him the terminus in his PV: a circular cavern. The stone walls had been smoothed. Writing had been engraved onto the wall. Imanol could not read it, but his link provided a translation: "Pilgrims bound for the

Temple of Hades, hold your key and implore the master of the underworld for entrance."

You've got to be kidding me. The Trilisks have been here a long time.

There, in the center of the room's floor, was a huge circular portal. It was made of some rust-free metal or ceramic. Though dirty, it was clearly made to last.

End of the line. With those Trilisks up there dead, how could I possibly get through this?

Imanol kept going to see for himself. He reached the end two minutes later. The room at the end had enough space for him to stand straight. He brushed himself off even though his shiny black Veer suit had an electrostatically clean surface. He swept his laser's illumination over the ancient room. The air was cool and dry. He scanned the rocky floor. No footprints.

It doesn't seem like those ones in the house were visiting this much. But they had to know about it?

Imanol walked around the sealed door. His link showed no services.

Trilisks probably just opened it with a thought… Open!

The door did not respond. Imanol pondered the obstacle.

What can I do? Search the house. Look for anything that could be the key this writing mentions.

Imanol sent two of his four attendants back up to the burned house. He instructed them to find anything interesting that survived the fire. While he waited, he cleared some of the sandy dirt from around the base. Imanol could not tell what it was made of. He thought about testing it with his laser, or even the rocket launcher.

If it's Trilisk, I'm not blasting through it.

An attendant above ground found an item in the house's ashes made of the same material. Imanol told it to bring the item back. Imanol guessed it would be the key.

Yet there was no place for a key anywhere on the surface of the portal. His attendants returned with the device.

Imanol held it in his hand. It was flat, cold, formed in a flat diamond shape. His link still showed no services. Imanol shook his head. It was not a Terran door, it was Trilisk.

Open! Open!

The remaining dirt on the portal's surface flew away in an instant. Now the portal looked brand new. Then the door made a loud grinding noise. The circular seal turned and slid away, revealing an enormous black opening. Warm, moist air belched upwards. It had an odor Imanol could not place.

Great. Just great.

Imanol checked his other light sources. He had a mini lantern, no larger than his thumb, which could light a small room. His stunner and the attendants also had small light sources. He told three attendants to slip down into the room below and help light the flanks.

At this point, if something is waiting for me, it'll be an easy shot if it's waiting in the dark.

Imanol tossed the mini lantern down for good measure. It fell about four meters to a smooth black surface below.

I need Telisa's eye, he thought. He knew her artificial eye could probably see very well in low light. *I wonder if she's still alive.*

Imanol finally decided to follow his attendants down. He considered the key. Leaving it here would help anyone else who showed up. But if there was an enemy survivor somewhere on the island, they could seal him in with it. He decided to bring the key with him and put it in his pack.

I hope it's tough. If I take a tumble and break it, that could suck... I'll leave the door open. When I leave, I'll have to stack something to climb on or throw a smart rope up there.

Imanol checked his pack and verified he had the rope. Then he looked down through the opening. The tunnel wall was perfectly smooth and utterly black. His attendants had not found any danger waiting for him.

If I were an ancient Greek, I'd believe this was the underworld, too.

Imanol decided to drop without his smart rope. It was not far to the floor below. He climbed to the edge, hung down by his hands as if doing a chin up, then released. He hit the ground and knelt to keep from falling backwards.

There was room for Imanol to stand inside the circular tunnel. The portal above dropped down into a tunnel running roughly north and south under the island. Two attendants flew away down the tunnel in opposite directions. As the attendants flew away, Imanol started to see that the tunnels extended farther than the island.

One of the attendants found a room. It was as large as a floor of the house above, filled with dark columns extending from floor to ceiling, though they did not seem structural. The other attendant had gone down a long descending tube. It saw a glow ahead. Imanol watched as the attendant flew closer. The tunnel above and beneath glowed a dull reddish light.

Imanol asked the attendant to do a radiation analysis, but it reported only slight visual red and infrared emissions.

What's causing that? Is there magma outside that tunnel?

Imanol recalled reading a report on his target island, which included notes of volcanic activity nearby. He shook his head.

To the Trilisks, even the scariest forces of nature are just a light show.

The attendants flew past several branchings, reporting more rooms and tunnels. They had not seen anything alive, or for that matter, any robots or active machines.

This is a major Trilisk complex!

Imanol decided he should report his 'success' and the Trilisk base. He was not supposed to contact any of the others directly. They had agreed to route communications through Cilreth to prevent any kind of tracking or interference by the Space Force.

"Cilreth? I suppose you can't tie me through to Telisa?"

There was nothing.

"Cilreth?"

Imanol felt a sense of dread. He was not supposed to contact anyone for at least twenty hours if Cilreth did not respond. By that time, the others would have succeeded or failed.

Someone said that Earth used to have a Trilisk base. Who was that? They said its AI wasn't working, like that meant something special. I guess that means the base is somehow without power or disabled in some way?

Imanol kept moving through the tunnel. He thought better of having two attendants exploring, so he sent for one to come back and instead stay about a hundred meters ahead of his route.

If it sees something bad, I guess I should shoot first and ask questions never.

Imanol headed toward what he suspected might be the center of the complex based upon the map his attendants had accumulated. He started to jog through the tunnel. It started to angle downwards. Imanol made good time. The optimum simultaneous strike time of the PIT mission had come and gone when he killed the Trilisks above. Any Trilisk left on Earth now had to know it was an endangered species.

The others must be well along now. If there's a Trilisk, it's probably heard the news. And I'm probably a dead man.

His lead attendant found something. A huge chamber. Imanol watched the video feed. There was a building inside the Trilisk base! The structure had the style of an ancient Greek temple. The attendant reported several life signs inside. Imanol recalled it back to his position to avoid notice. He arranged for the remaining scout to return to him as well. Imanol wanted all the protection he could get.

I can't believe how long this thing has been down here. The Trilisks made a temple down here for the natives? I thought they just observed other races from these complexes. Or used them as hosts for fun, or something secret. But looks like they played the deity card on the poor bastards.

Imanol readied his weapons. Before he made it to the end of the last tunnel leading to the temple building, all four attendants orbited him, ready to help. He had to run through the glowing tunnel his attendant had found. Imanol ignored the glow and what it probably meant.

If I'm going to go deep into this complex hunting Trilisks, I can't let a little magma get to me.

He could not tell if the tunnel was hotter or if it was just his imagination. His suit was a good insulator, too. The reddish glow faded behind him to be replaced by a yellowish one ahead. He could see in his PV he was almost to the large temple chamber.

Finally Imanol emerged from the tunnel and got his first look with his own eyes. The room was big and black. The building looked like it had been built on the surface of an asteroid hurling through deep space. It was lit from inside. Imanol wondered how long that light had been on.

This is utterly insane.

Imanol stared. He traced the distinctive lines of ancient architecture. The materials were wrong. The temple was not built from stone. It was made of the same dark, almost indestructible material as the Trilisk walls which towered overhead. There were lines in its surface, as if it had been put together from separate pieces, but Imanol suspected they were fake. But the lines of the temple were Greek.

They built this to impress the locals. I bet it worked, too.

Imanol caught sight of something at the base of the structure. He walked carefully forward to get a look.

There, sitting at the bottom of the wide stair leading up to the temple, a man in leather tunic and sandals sat with a circular shield and a spear beside him. Piles of bones sat around him. They looked ancient.

"Blood and souls," Imanol whispered in awe.

Chapter 17

A Vovokan shuttle hurtled through space toward Earth.

Inside, Cilreth2 took a deep breath and tried to center herself. Her insides roiled like a tornado of knives. She wanted to scream.

She needed twitch. Fast.

When she had come out of the Trilisk column she had felt better than ever before. And she had assumed the benefits of an immortal body would include an immunity from the slow damage of twitch. When she tried some, the twitch had affected her more than when she was human. To Cilreth2, twitch was like a rocket ride, a combination of cerebral nitro and opium-like euphoria. She had been taken by surprise from the beginning, and two days later she was addicted ten times harder than Cilreth. She didn't share this terrible development with her original. Cilreth2 was supposed to be super strong, super smart, and bulletproof. She had wondered what it said about her personality that she would not share this problem with herself.

Luckily, she had an opportunity to fix all this up in one day.

I hope my slow self hasn't noticed I'm gone yet. She'll know by the time I get back.

A little quick research had allowed her to catch up with an old friend, Nell. Or was Nell an old enemy? When it came to a drug supplier, the words could blend together quickly. Her supplier had been someone who had given her a steady stream of the drug whenever she needed it, never ratted her out, and kept her supply of twitch pure and safe. But Cilreth had learned the hard way that when it came to money, people had less friends than they thought. Cilreth2 had every memory of it.

Nell had moved up a notch in the supply chain since the original Cilreth left Earth. She operated out of a nice mansion outside of Phoenix, where Cilreth had lived before moving to the frontier. Even then Nell had had long silvery hair, though Cilreth wasn't sure if it was from endless twitch usage or just an affectation.

Cilreth2's spacecraft was, of course, utterly illegal to fly anywhere in the system, being unregistered, stealthy, armed, without logging protocols, and of course, alien. The Space Force would throw her in jail for a lifetime, should they ever find out about it and catch her. But Cilreth2 could not care in her current condition. She just needed a lot of twitch.

She had considered approaching Maxsym with the problem several times. But the bottom line was that Maxsym's loyalty to PIT was high. They were providing him with everything he needed. Anyway, Cilreth2 thought there was a good chance Maxsym would think it was a test. He would report it to the others one way or the other.

She came in toward Phoenix directly. The gravity spinner allowed her to avoid the complexities of reentry experienced by pilots of previous centuries. Soon she had a lock on the house she sought.

The Vovokan shuttle was strong and light, an amazing piece of technology. The target mansion specs showed her it would hold the weight of her craft with a lot to spare. She brought it down. The bottom of the craft extended a malleable force field to hold the shuttle above the roof. The invisible field molded itself to the shape of the roof, putting equal pressure across the entire surface. Just another miracle of Vovokan technology.

I wonder if they heard that. Must have been some creaking.

Cilreth2 picked up a stubby assault weapon and shrugged. She did not care that much if they heard her coming. She would try asking for what she wanted first, but she knew it would get rough fast. For them. With her withdrawal symptoms raging, her patience was at an all time low.

She had two attendants with her. She was trying to decide whether she needed them when she had second thoughts about her approach. She discarded the assault weapon. She had not thought this through carefully. No point in going in shooting. Concealed weapons is what she wanted. Luckily she had brought more than enough of an arsenal with her, just in case. She grabbed two pistols and a sword. She smiled. The sword would give her a certain air of business. They would laugh at it, until they saw how fast the new Cilreth was. The pistols were almost antique 10mm weapons, but in solid working order.

When you're a perfect shot with super-fast reflexes, best to trade off magazine capacity for stopping power, she thought. Modern pistols all used ultra high velocity rounds of tiny caliber that gave a much higher magazine count and helped to cut down on unnecessary death. Most of them could deliver a paralytic poison and be used as *almost* non-lethal weapons. By comparison, her 10mms were field cannons. They would blow off limbs. That suited her mood just fine. Let them spend a couple of months regrowing an arm or two.

Cilreth2 disembarked through a hatch on a smart rope. She dropped down smoothly and tried a window. It was not locked. Cilreth2 paused, looking at the pocked weather coating and the aged roof cleaning machine, which sat idle to her right.

Still not spending money on your surroundings, I see, Cilreth2 thought. She let herself in.

Once inside, her perspective changed. She felt a little more like her old self and less like a superhero. She found herself in an upstairs bathroom that she vaguely remembered from Cilreth's time here. The familiar smell of spiral filled the air. Spiral was a mirror drug to twitch, the downer to the upper. Some people wanted to function faster, others wanted to unwind and slow down time.

Cilreth2 used her heightened senses to listen to the house. She heard at least five people moving inside. That was in line with the old days. Nell knew she was safer with an entourage. In addition to her soldiers, she would have one or two close companions and a variable number of clients in the house at any given time. Cilreth2 might even be able to walk right in and out without notice.

She cracked the door and peeked. Then she shrugged.

I don't have time for this. I'll wake Cthulhu if I have to. Gimme my twitch.

Cilreth walked out into the hall. She followed the hall, found a staircase, and walked down. She saw Nell in the great room at the bottom of the stairs. Nell looked older, of course, with some new face wrinkles to go with her silver hair. She wore a warm but rugged looking green overshirt with tights over her legs. Tread patches built into the leggings served as her shoes.

There was a guard with a rifle on his shoulder, behind a couch that held Nell and two other women. He looked young, brave and stupid, with long black hair and the beginnings of a beard. The other women were younger, and obviously preened themselves with an eye toward being noticed. They wore tight clothing with a shifting translucent patch that moved over their bodies.

No one looked at her for a second or two. Then the guard caught sight of Cilreth2. He got a concerned look on his face. He touched Nell on the shoulder and indicated the newcomer.

Nell's eyebrows went up. Then she smiled.

She's shocked, but covering well.

"Wow. A blast from the past. Cilreth. It's been a while, minnow."

"You owe me some twitch. With interest," Cilreth2 said. The guard bristled a bit at her tone, but he remained overconfident.

"How's that?" Nell asked. She smiled. She was still striking. Her silver hair went surprisingly well on a face of mixed British and Chinese heritage.

"I paid you a year's worth of Cit2Cit creds as you recall. Then I had to leave it behind. You made a nice profit off me."

Nell shrugged. "Not my fault you had to leave. Business. You know that."

"Give me your twitch," Cilreth2 said slowly. The threat part went unsaid.

Nell's bodyguard began to move around the couch toward the stair. Another guard approached from a side door. Their hands found the handles of their weapons.

Nell perked up. She thrived on action. That was probably how she got into this profession in the first place.

"No," Nell said.

Time to teach her action is not always of the fun variety. If she can learn the lesson without dying.

Her amped nervous system had her moving before the guards could react. Her 10mms flicked out.

Blam! Blam!

Cilreth2 put a round in each bodyguard's forehead before anyone could move. Before they could fall, Cilreth2 had Nell in both her fire cones. But another guard appeared on a balcony above. Cilreth had one weapon aimed upwards in a fraction of a second.

Blam!

The guard above fell back out of sight. One of Cilreth2's guns remained trained on Nell. Cilreth2's attendants sought out more combatants. They found three more within as many seconds, but these ones were taking it slow, waiting.

*So much for the idea of making them regrow limbs.
Unless medical technology has taken a leap forward and
they can regrow heads now.*

"Live or die," Cilreth2 said. The lack of twitch had her
nerves grating. It took a lot of willpower to keep from just
blowing Nell away on the spot as a release of frustration.

Nell smiled. But an attendant reported to Cilreth2 that
her heart rate was rapid.

"Okay, I hear you," Nell said. "We'll get you what's
yours."

"With interest," Cilreth2 said. "I know you still have
more friends in the house. Any more attempts to kill me,
and you're not going to make it."

Nell nodded. Cilreth2 knew she would be talking with
her friends among their links.

"Okay, I'm sending someone to bring it. Don't shoot
her."

"I will, if she has a weapon," Cilreth2 warned.

Cilreth2 tried to watch everything at once. She had her
own vision and the feeds from two attendants to process.
She could also hear almost everything going on in the
house. One attendant kept rotating its view of the three
armed people she knew about, while another kept tabs on a
woman who was retrieving her twitch. Even with her fast
reflexes it taxed her.

I should have trained more with the PIT guys recently.

The attendant settled on one guard who was behind
Cilreth2 in the house. He was moving out, getting ready to
shoot her from behind. Cilreth2 stepped back from Nell
and turned one outstretched arm holding a pistol in a wide
arc to cover the doorway at her left flank. She fired just
before the tenuous sound of footsteps reached the
doorway.

Blam! Blam!

Her two rounds went through the doorframe and hit
the guard before he even came out into the open. His body

fell out into the room, sending his weapon clattering across the faux wood floor.

Nell noted the ease with which Cilreth2 had dispatched the attack. Nell's lips thinned and she frowned.

"Where did you learn to fight like that?"

"I've been gone a while, Nell. Give me what I want, no tricks, and you can make it through this. But I'm not keeping you alive for old times' sake."

"Okay. The bag is here, behind me. She's unarmed," Nell said, stepping slowly aside and indicating the door behind her.

"Send her in," Cilreth2 said calmly.

A woman with curly black hair came in. Her eyes were wide. An attendant told Cilreth2 this person was genuinely terrified. Cilreth2 covered her with a 10mm anyway.

The attendant scanned the bag. It did indeed contain twitch, but there was a hand grenade buried at the bottom. Cilreth2 took the bag, then tossed it aside. She shook her head.

"I warned you."

Cilreth holstered her right firearm. She reached for her sword. Nell started to say something, but it turned into a scream as Cilreth2's sword sliced through the bridge of her nose, sending blood into her eyes. Another of Nell's armed companions came out of cover from the kitchen door.

Blam!

The guard fell, dead.

Arms. You're supposed to be aiming for arms.

Cilreth2 put an attendant on the last armed combatant, but it saw the person withdraw. It was a young man in a vat-leather jacket. He was headed for the back door. Nell lay on the floor, muttering.

Cilreth2 told the attendants out to watch for danger while she searched for more twitch. It would not do for a survivor to shoot her in the back before she could escape with her prize.

She found what she needed in the same room it used to be. Cilreth2 silently thanked Nell for being a creature of habit. Large plastic barrels of twitch lay across one wall. One would be fake, a trap. She called an attendant in to make sure.

Yes. It's the same one. It sprays paralytic poison if you try to open it.

She grabbed two of the heavy containers and hauled them up to the roof. The house still had some clients, cowering in the bedrooms and one in a hall closet.

I wonder if they'll call the cops. I imagine they would have to be pretty scared to do that, but, people have died here. I'd better hurry.

Cilreth2 grabbed two more containers. They strained her enhanced musculature. She wasn't sure the original Cilreth could have lifted one, much less taken it all the way up to the shuttle on the roof. She decided to go for one last batch.

Who knows how long it will be before I can get more? And I can hardly just ask Maxsym to make me some. Unless he owed me a favor… I'll have to think on that.

Cilreth2 got her last load. Some of the clients were finally starting to peek out of their rooms. She ignored them. The sounds of Nell crying filtered up from downstairs. Her attendants were on her tail as she left the house for the last time and dropped her barrels in the cargo bay. Cilreth2 activated her shuttle and lifted from the roof before she hit the pilot's chair.

Problem solved, she thought to herself as her craft rose above the green estate and lifted into orbit. She could not wait any longer. She hopped into the back and gave herself a strong dose.

Cilreth2 let out a long hiss of satisfaction as the twitch hit her souped up nervous system.

"R'lyeh risen! Mission successful. We won't need more for a long time."

In the cargo hold behind her, half a metric ton of twitch lent weight to her conviction.

For the rest of the ride back, Cilreth2 worked hard to suppress the guilt that came from the bodies she had left behind.

Michael McCloskey

Chapter 18

Siobhan watched her copy head toward the house. The duplicate slipped out of sight suddenly, as if activating a stealth suit.

Frackjammers.

The other Siobhan had to be moving in on a mission of her own. If copied perfectly, the other version would also put the death of Spero above all else. So she might as well try to coordinate her efforts. The other one was going in. She should too.

"I can work with it," she told herself.

Siobhan gave the signal for stage two.

All around the island, soldier bots responded to her call. They moved sluggishly through the clear green waters and started to emerge onto the beach. Siobhan gave them orders to ignore other PIT soldiers or scouts they saw; it would make sense to assume they belonged to the other Siobhan.

Siobhan2 or Siobhan3? She wondered. *How far could the count possibly go?*

She headed straight for the wing of the compound opposite the one where she had seen her copy go. The design of the house suggested her copy's side was where Spero might sleep, which was exactly why Siobhan had targeted the other wing. She wanted to scare him out, not confront him where he was strongest. The other Siobhan was either working under Spero's control, or else did not care.

Siobhan realized if she encountered her superior self, she would have to shoot.

Chances are, she'll shoot first. She's faster. This is beyond dangerous.

She imagined living as a Trilisk slave. Obeying the Trilisk's orders with no hope of escape, until the Trilisk decided to kill her.

*Or maybe a duplicate would just be an extra body. The
Trilisk would keep you around always, as a backup place
to live. Maybe that's why the duplicate bodies can always
be controlled. So that Trilisks can have an entourage that
serves as a reserve of hosts in case their current host dies.
Or becomes boring.*

Siobhan came to the compound wall. It was over ten
meters tall, with a tan hue that suggested the concrete had
been mixed from the local sand. She slowed. She knew
this was the kind of place a death trap could be set for
invisible trespassers.

*A Vovokan would set up a mass detector with a bomb
or a laser. What would a Trilisk do?*

Siobhan decided if she wanted to rattle the inhabitants,
she might as well start making noise. She drew her
Vovokan weapon. She targeted ten places on the wall, all
around the entire compound. Then she started shooting.
One by one, she sent mech rounds into the wall. The noise
of the hits started to echo across the island.

She stood outside the seventh spot on the list. No one
would know which one to cover. The round blasted a huge
hole right through the barrier. She was impressed by the
awesome firepower of her Vovokan weapon, and yet, the
robot had not been touched by it.

Make them cover all ten. Or try.

Siobhan routed her soldiers toward each breach. Then
she ran through the hole she had created. The barrier had
been meters thick; she felt vulnerable going through but
she made it to the inside alive. The sounds of war
continued across the island. From inside the wall, Siobhan
spotted turrets atop the defenses shooting at her soldiers.
She used her dispersed attendants to spot them, then
started shooting again. She sent six more mech rounds into
turrets atop the wall.

Siobhan saw that turrets on the far side were emitting
smoke and debris.

I guess my duplicate is doing some shooting of her own. Did Shiny give her all the same equipment?

Siobhan approached the mansion. A beautiful set of huge double doors led into the wing. They looked massive. Possibly even made of thick steel beneath their carved exteriors.

A random thought flitted through Siobhan's brain at that moment.

Am I a duplicate, too?

She suppressed the doubt.

Who cares as long as I get Spero? Then I can look into how Shiny used me. I wonder if he expects me to die. If I kill the Trilisk I should ditch the weapon and the suit; maybe they are designed to dispose of me later.

Siobhan let Shiny's control device scan the door's interface. Vulnerabilities came up. The device told her link it had unlocked the door and disabled two security alarms. Siobhan knew there would be hidden cameras; that did not concern her since she was in an improved stealth suit.

So the robot has superior security. Perhaps it is made by Trilisks? Though it could not see me…

Siobhan's link told the doors to open and they did. She told a grenade to take off into the mansion. It obeyed quickly. Once away from her, it became visible. The grenade scouted the interior for her: it saw a long hallway leading to the atrium of the wing. There were no more obvious obstacles, so she told the grenade to detonate in the atrium.

Krumpf.

All part of the show. You're under attack. Get ready to run for it.

Siobhan had the attendants surrounding the island ready to flag anything unusual. She had gained confidence in the plan. If the Trilisk had any of its old power, she would probably already be dead. She now felt she was dealing with a cowardly Trilisk immortal that did not have any of the powers of its ancestors. That meant it had an escape plan or two. She hoped there was not something like a tunnel to a submarine hangar. That might actually get Spero out alive.

Siobhan stood at the edge of the wing. She advanced into the building, toward the heart of the compound. Past the damaged atrium, she saw a strongpoint where the wing connected to the next section of the building. It had a security station and a dark laser dome in the ceiling.

Paranoid around here. The compound has been sectioned off into zones with security stations between them. What's wrong, Spero? Can't trust the help?

Outside, Siobhan had lost a lot of soldiers. The distraction of the outside attack had a timer on it. Still, Spero did not leave the building. She hesitated. Should she stay in here and keep pecking away, or go outside and try to destroy more defenses from there? She decided the Trilisk would be more likely to run if it knew it was being attacked both inside and outside the house.

Siobhan launched a mech round into a laser emplacement above the strongpoint.

Kaboom!

The entire checkpoint erupted in sparks. For a moment her view of the corridor was obscured by smoke. She moved cautiously forward.

A tall shadow formed in the smoke. Siobhan halted. The shadow resolved into a large robot. Her blood ran cold. It was the same one she had narrowly avoided outside. Or at least the same model. It headed right for her.

The gray metal armor gleamed. The edges of its head, shoulders, and feet were trimmed in red. It hovered just over the floor. Siobhan shivered as the barrels of its weapons swept over her. As long as those red eyes scanned back and forth, she did not dare move.

Siobhan heard a periodic hiss of air. She looked at the machine. She saw air slits in its chest.

Is it breathing? Or sniffing? One thing's for sure: it's searching for me.

Siobhan retreated down the hall. The thing did not shoot at her. At least for now, it had not spotted her.

Screw the plan. Who am I kidding? I'm going in after the bastard and I'll be damned if any frackjammin robot is going to stop me.

Siobhan reversed course. She walked toward it. She felt the familiar thrill of danger hit her system. Some part of her knew what she was doing was not smart, that she was out of control. Those thoughts were not allowed to surface. Instead, she reveled in the adrenal hit.

Her Vovokan weapon came up and started shooting mech rounds. She listened watched the magazine count drop in her PV as she ran toward it as if in slow motion: 31, 30, 29…

Boom, boom, boom.

Shrapnel engulfed the robot. Siobhan saw scratches appear in the armor. The rounds were not hitting it, but the flying debris were. The walls around the robot were shredded. Somewhere to her right a water pipe burst and added its spray to the chaos.

Any closer and I'm going to get a face full of shrapnel myself.

The machine returned fire down the hallway. The entire corridor erupted as if it had been filled with explosives. Siobhan dropped to the floor. She felt debris striking her suit. The floor beneath her shook. Her suit reported no serious damage. The machine had not hit her directly.

She tried to stitch rounds at the robot's legs from a prone firing position.

28, 27, 26, 25…

Brroom, boom, boom, boom.

Dammit Shiny, you said this hi tech noise was supposed to work…

Siobhan stopped shooting as she lost track of the target in thick smoke. The black cloud flowed down the hallway and engulfed her. She breathed from her suit's reserve. She waited for the robot to reappear. She lay utterly still for long seconds with nothing but sooty ash flurrying in front of her face mask. Finally, it started to clear. Then she saw it. One meter directly above her.

She pointed her weapon and told it to fire again.

Krumpf!

The machine exploded above her. Siobhan felt a sharp pain. For a moment she languished, blind and hurt. A piece of the machine fell, pinning her legs. Her faceplate was damaged. She took a deep breath from the oxygen reserve and lifted the visor to take a peek.

She looked down at herself. Instead of the outline of her body supplied by the suit when she was invisible, she saw her damaged stealth suit in plain sight. It was not working. A piece of metal stuck out of her chest, oozing blood.

Frackjammers.

Chapter 19

"I need ideas. Crazy ones," Sager demanded.

Ten of his officers had assembled incarnate to decide on a plan of action. Sager was insistent upon that point—*action*—and they were running out of time.

"They might be listening to us," Officer Claren noted. Claren was in charge of the powerful weapons of the *Bismarck*, now held in a state of power starvation by the aliens using means unknown.

"Fight or escape?" Sager said.

"Escape," Claren said.

Narron nodded. "We can't see them. We can't power up weapons past a small fraction of power. Presumably the enemy has point defenses and enough power to destroy us in one alpha strike. A surprise escape is our best hope."

"We have the *Marco Polo*," Officer Jackson said. She spoke quietly, but Sager knew from experience she had ideas worth listening to.

"What can we do with it?" Narron said.

"We could blow it up. Use it for a distraction," someone said.

"Maybe the explosion energy or debris could help us detect the enemy ships."

"We could escape on it. Use a diversion here," an officer added.

"We can't give up this ship, it's the newest battleship we have!" another officer said.

"What kind of diversions can we make?" Sager asked. "The energy rings on the gravity spinner and the weapons won't charge up past ten percent power."

"We could turn our power off."

"We could blow up our drive. Not really. Just start the process. Tell them we're killing ourselves. Then do something else."

"We could feign an emergency and get them to let the power through."

"An emergency doesn't require the spinner or the weapons."

"The *Marco Polo* has a gravity spinner, too," Jackson said. "It could be used on *Bismarck*."

"It has the same power limitations," Narron said.

"Okay, this is workable," a drive engineer named Tell said. "We can pretend we want to blow ourselves up as someone mentioned. We'll go to maximum power output, as we did when we were testing this trap earlier. Both ships at once. We'll get all the rings on both ships up to ten percent. At the last moment, we reroute all the rings, on the weapons and the gravity spinner, into the gravity spinners on both ships. The *Marco Polo* won't try to translate itself. Its gravity spinner will focus on *Bismarck* as Jackson suggested. Both gravity spinners and all the rings might get us to thirty percent of normal jump power. But once we've jumped away, we should be able to get all our power to the spinner and jump again immediately."

Sager nodded. "Raigel. What do you think of our chances with that plan?"

"Hard to calculate," the cold voice responded. "Perhaps ten percent."

Sager actually felt happy. He had not heard Raigel give any plan more than a one percent chance since they had been captured.

"Tell our captors we have new demands," Sager ordered. "We must be released now, or else we're going to scuttle both ships. Tell, get the sequence for both jumps together. Everyone, get the rings ready to reroute. You have to get it right, no testing. I don't want to tip our hand by sending any power down unusual routes until we make our attempt."

***

Caden had just about given up. There was not much more action he would be seeing from the inside of the holding room, and it did not look like he would be released anytime soon.

Suddenly the floor shuddered. The interrogator cursed.

"What's that?" Caden asked. His link was isolated. It told him nothing.

"The attack has reached us," the man said. "Haven't you been listening? Sol System is under assault."

"The attack on the outer system is just a diversion," Caden said. "No one is really being hurt. Just cut off. Those transmissions aren't real. It's all manufactured."

Yet Caden doubted himself.

Sol System is under assault. I thought I would never hear such terrible words.

"You're delusional," his interrogator said. His eyes unfocused.

"If those spheres make it in here, I'm going to make sure they find you dead."

Caden's eyes grew wide. "What spheres? You'll shoot me? I'm on your side! Are you talking about the little gray spheres that came with me? They're harmless. I used them to find—"

Caden got a pointer. He tried to connect to Cilreth. His link was still isolated. He could only access what Bailey wanted him to see.

An image feed opened in his mind's eye. A spherical Vovokan assault drone the size of a land car flew through a shuttle bay. Its shields glowed in two or three spots. Caden assumed it was getting hit by high frequency lasers invisible to his eyes. As he watched the drone traded fire with a military robot and a handful of Space Force marines. The sphere dodged two missiles, then reduced its opponents to ash.

"It's not just here. Even the *Bismarck* is missing in action," Bailey said in dismay.

"No! No… that's not the plan. This is all wrong."

The Vovokan drone in Caden's PV burned through a bulkhead and melted two more robots in its way. Bailey looked at Caden. He was suddenly very sad. "Maybe you believe that, son. You've been used by aliens. You probably never had a chance to see the truth, until now."

Could this all be an act? He's kind of showing a lot of dismay for someone conducting an interrogation. You're supposed to keep your cool, demonstrate dominance and control. I believe him… they gave me drugs, though. I can't trust anything. It's social engineering.

"Oh no… no," Bailey said.

Could it get worse?

"What?" Caden asked.

"Skyhold. The aliens have destroyed it."

Telisa!

"Look, this is crazy, but, I came to take out one kind of alien, but these battle spheres are from another alien. It was supposed to be on our side." Caden dropped his head. He had failed the Space Force, failed his parents, failed all of Earth.

How could this happen? I wanted to be a hero. Now I'm what… the biggest traitor in history?

"Where is this alien? We have to kill it," Bailey said.

A trick? Maybe. What difference does it make? They can't hurt Shiny.

"It's on a huge spaceship the size of Space Force Command. An advanced space ship. We have no hope without Cilreth."

"Who?"

Caden perked up. "Cilreth! A friend of mine… she has control of one of the ships! If we can contact her, we might be able to get her to help us."

Bailey watched the spheres burn through a hardpoint. Sweat ran down his face.

"Talk to whoever you want," Bailey said. "It's over."

"Cilreth!" Caden sent out. "Cilreth!"

There was no answer.

Caden contacted his attendants. The machines responded. They had escaped when Caden was captured. They reported all three suspected Trilisks had been killed. They verified that SFC was under attack, but they could not communicate with the larger Trilisk arsenal attacking the station. Caden recalled them.

I may need them just to survive. If they don't turn on me.

Bailey opened the door to the room and left. He left the door wide open.

Could this be a virtual trick? Caden thought. The Space Force probably has the ability to override people's links. This isn't real. Right. So I should not be giving away secrets. My link is probably showing them how to talk to the Vovokan attendants, if nothing else.

Caden left the room. He was in some kind of security station. The first of his attendants flitted toward him. He reached for a weapon that was not there at his belt. A huge amount of noise came to this link as he re-accessed Space Force Command.

"Abandon ship. Abandon ship. Follow your shuttle evac lines."

"There's one coming for Central Security!" a soldier transmitted.

"We have two lasers and five Tiger Twelves. We can't stop it."

More vibrations came through the station. This time the rumbling did not stop.

"Aigis isn't replying! Aigis is offline!"

Central Security... that's where I am now!

145

Caden swallowed hard. A bright red line flickered in his mind's eye, directing him to the nearest evac bay. The deck shook again, violently. Gravity cut out from under him.

Caden reacted. There would be enough time to wonder later. He brought tucked his knees up, then pushed off as he spun into line with the corridor with his red escape line.

Is this real?

Thoughts of what was happening and his part in it submerged as Caden fought to survive.

Chapter 20

The attendants circling Imanol gave warning. Multiple Trilisk signatures had been detected within the vicinity of the eerie temple, including the man before him.

The man gasped. He stood shakily. The man looked extremely thin, almost skeletal. His face was gaunt and sunken. Then he screamed several unfamiliar words hoarsely. The man snatched up his spear and shield.

Imanol could not catch the meaning. His link provided a translation: "The portal! The way is open!"

"Oh no you don't, incomalcon," Imanol said, backing up and drawing two pistols. Imanol shot as the ancient being before him threw its spear. Imanol tried to dodge, but the throw was well aimed. Imanol's Veer suit deflected the projectile. The man fell at the same time as his spear. Blood poured from the wound caused by a projectile impact.

"That was hardly a superhuman attack," Imanol said aloud. "Not that I'm complaining."

Imanol charged up the stairs, weapons ready. He held his laser pistol in his right hand and a projectile pistol in his left. The dark surfaces of the temple made the shadows tricky. He slowed at the top, trying to discern the niches of the architecture. He decided nothing lurked within his vision.

Inside the temple, Imanol saw more columns, but these were different. Tubes and lights were scattered across their upper quarter. They looked like taller versions of the other Trilisk columns, the ones they had used to duplicate themselves. Imanol checked his flanks. He saw another man in ancient garb advancing on him from the left with a chipped sword. At the same time, he heard a noise behind him.

Imanol ran toward the enemy he could see and shot him with his slug pistol. Then he spun, putting his back toward a Trilisk column. Two more unhealthy-looking men advanced. They held spears and one had a shield.

One yelled something. "Kill him!" his link translated.

Imanol tried to shoot both at once. Thanks to the enhanced targeting of his smart weapons, he was able to hit both of them simultaneously. One of the spears came toward him, but this time an attendant deflected it. The men fell to the ground. One of them moaned.

Imanol walked over to the one he knew was still alive.

"How long? How long have you been here?" he demanded.

The man stared ahead but Imanol could not tell if he saw anything. Imanol's attendants emitted a translation of Imanol's question. Blood poured out of the chest of his fallen attacker.

The man uttered something, then weakly coughed up more blood.

Imanol's link provided a translation, labeled at 85% likely: "Forever".

This is insane. If they want out, why don't they just run for it?

Imanol saw a long table on the other side of a black dais set between several columns at the center of the temple.

It was clearly a dining table. The plates were empty. Given the state of the men that had attacked him, Imanol did not find that surprising. The number of bones everywhere made him suspect cannibalism.

So their base down here shuts down, they run out of food... and they start eating each other. But it's been thousands of years... unless the Trilisk bodies are a hell of a lot tougher than I thought.

Imanol had the impression that the super-bodies needed more calories, not less.

It's so dark in here. The walls absorb my light. I wish I could see better, he thought.

148

The illumination in the temple rose feebly.

Imanol did a double-take. *I want it darker.*

The light receded. Imanol was plunged into darkness. Only the light from his weapon shone across the temple.

Wow. Light, please.

The light slowly returned. Imanol caught movement out of the corner of his eye. He spun to confront whatever moved.

It was a Trilisk.

Imanol felt an instinctual fear of the unknown rise and grip him. It was not terrifying because of the awesome technology the Trilisks had wielded. It was just an awful monstrous thing. Imanol stared at the three legs, three arms, and the hideous shape of its body, looking just enough like a giant face to be deeply disturbing.

Imanol's laser came up and fired. He yelled something unintelligible. The thing turned, smoke coming from its side, showing him another grotesque face, one gray eye, cold like a giant squid eye, with a mouth or gill slit underneath. The laser fired again, putting another hole into the body. The thing kept coming, bouncing into Imanol and bowling him over. Imanol yelled in disgust and fear again. An attendant smashed into one of its legs, emitting a grotesque crunching sound.

Imanol had thought of the slit beneath its eye as a mouth, but now he was on the floor he saw its real mouth, a triple-tusked maw on the underside between the three legs. Before Imanol could shoot again, it bit him on the leg.

Imanol screamed. He set the laser to double energy and shot again and again. Finally it stopped moving. His laser reported an overheated condition. Imanol ignored it and pushed the Trilisk's limbs away with his legs.

Imanol spasmed. He tried to stand but just fell back, shaking violently.

"Get it together! Get it together you incomalcon!" he yelled at himself. The thing was so weird, so ugly, his reaction was a hundred times worse than if a large crocodile had appeared and tried to eat him. Imanol had never shaken so much. He watched his own hands quivering and willed them to stop.

It's like living a horror VR. I think I could make a good horror VR now.

Somehow the thought struck him as funny. Part of his shock wore off. He laughed a bit even as he spit vomit out of his mouth. "Yeah, I'll make a bloody horror simulation and get rich. Just get rich and sit around doing nothing. No more ancient temples."

He checked his leg. The Veer suit had protected him from most of the damage. Only the tusks had penetrated it. Some blood had leaked out, but the suit had sterilized the wound and sealed him up automatically.

Bitten by a Trilisk. Bitten! It was nothing more than a savage. A primitive monster.

Imanol still shook. He felt ill. He thought of poison for a moment, then just told himself it was just his mental reaction to the attack. The Trilisk had acted like a rabid dog, not a member of a super race that had dominated their section of the galaxy.

It must have been trapped down here for hundreds… or thousand of years? How could they survive? They have starved… but even an augmented body would have to eat in this time?

Imanol considered the piles of bones.

Well they didn't all survive. Maybe the columns provided limited food and water which they had to fight over? Or maybe they figured out how to grow some food. Something down here still works a little bit. It gave me light. Kind of. No wonder they're all mad as loons though.

"Cilreth? Can you hear me?"

Imanol received no reply. He was on his own.

He considered the situation. The Trilisk base was large; there could be more Trilisks hiding in here. On the other hand, they clearly were not in any shape to threaten Earth. And he had had enough slaughter for one day. He felt the key in his pack.

Maybe I should talk it over with Cilreth?

He felt like he might be second guessing himself. He did not want to continue killing these things. But that was his mission. Was he dodging out on his part of the plan?

No. They aren't a threat like we thought. I should ask the team what to do about them. Maybe we could take them prisoner and learn from them.

He decided to head back to the surface and check if he could raise Cilreth from there. He sent one attendant ahead to check the entrance and see if anyone or anything had escaped. Then he took a deep breath and walked away from the Temple of Hades.

Michael McCloskey

Chapter 21

Siobhan awakened. She coughed.

I'm dying!

She opened her eyes. Her lungs burned. She coughed again. Looking at the jagged metal sticking out of her, she thought she must be coughing up blood.

Her suit was malfunctioning, but she was able to manually switch to an isolated oxygen supply. She breathed deeply. She could not feel any bubbling in her lung.

The metal had not pierced her lung. She grabbed it and pulled it out. Then she screamed in pain. She rolled over, got her hands and feet under her and stood up. She staggered back into a wall. Blood poured out of the wound in her chest, so she pulled her pack around and grabbed a medical sealant. She wiped the blood clear and sprayed it over quickly. The sealant staunched the flow of blood.

That's good. The gas… oh. If that was poison, I'm dead anyway.

Siobhan felt ill, but it was not severe. The gas was definitely not pleasant.

I'm just having a psychosomatic reaction to it, she told herself. *If it was real poison I would have dropped like a fly in a stunner cone.*

Siobhan tried to fight it off. She still found it odd that the substance could nauseate her so thoroughly and yet it was not something deadly meant to kill her.

Maybe just luck. Maybe I only caught a few molecules of something really lethal.

Siobhan's link told her that her stealth suit had failed. She started to laugh. It was a bit late to the party. She realized she had no weapon. Shiny's device lay on the floor pitted with debris. She walked over and retrieved it. Her link could not reach it. She saw it had been damaged, but not much.

I suppose it could explode if damaged. I already narrowly lived through one explosion.

Siobhan holstered the Vovokan weapon. She grabbed her shock baton from her belt. The weapon had no range, but it had one overwhelming advantage: it would feel great to brain Spero with it. Siobhan stood up. The gash in the front of her suit was a dangerous weakness: a single projectile in the right spot would kill her.

Siobhan sent her surviving attendant through to the other wing. She staggered after it. She had to find Spero now, because with Shiny's weapon on the fritz, she would not be able to stop him if he fled.

Should I call the outside ones in, too? No. I need to know if he leaves, track him.

All of her soldier robots were dead. That meant, unless it had been a perfect draw, there were still some Spero security forces somewhere. Siobhan hoped that did not include another of those killer robots. If she ran into one of those, she would soon learn if Shiny's weapon was disabled, because activating it would be her only hope.

The attendant passed through vast rooms in the center of the compound. These were places for impressing guests: beautiful dining rooms, atriums, and VR parlors. A long balcony overlooking the ocean. Two hallways with a dozen guest bedrooms.

The attendant found a destroyed checkpoint. Blood bespattered the walls. Someone had been killed there.

Spero?

The attendant flew on. Siobhan walked through a wide room with a tiled floor covered in robot parts. More things had died here. There were burn marks but no blood.

She heard a yell from her video feed. A man with silver hair in an exercise suit ran feebly from the attendant. He had some kind of a mask over his face. Something was wrong with his skin.

The attendant identified him as a Trilisk host body.

Spero.

She redoubled her pace, though it hurt, headed toward him. The attendant shadowed him, but then its feed went dead. Siobhan left caution to the wind. She was so close, and out of time. She had to finish him before anything big showed up.

She climbed up stairs and advanced in a crouch toward the room where the attendant had followed Spero. From her position, it looked like an old fashioned office.

Siobhan saw his leg protruding from part of a big desk.

Frackjammers. It would have been nice to have an excuse.

She took a deep breath and entered the room. She felt another rush of adrenaline. Her hand flexed on the handle of the shock baton. Through her link, she told the weapon to discharge its entire energy reserve in the next strike: a lethal dose, even for a superhuman.

Siobhan felt no fear, even though his pistol could inflict lethal damage. She had the shock baton ready. Siobhan charged the desk. She came over the top of it and saw him.

In one instant her brain registered the scene: a man in a gas mask, his face oozing clear liquid and blood from his exposed skin around the mask, struggling to target her with his pistol in a bloodied hand.

The baton arced down onto Spero's head. Blood sprayed across the wall holding fake books. Siobhan blinked.

"That was for my family," she said.

Michael McCloskey

Chapter 22

Telisa tipped her head. Telisa3 crouched directly across from her, covering behind a counter. They each wore the green circle jumpsuit of an android. Telisa had her Veer suit underneath, and Telisa3 wore a Shiny-enhanced stealth suit under hers.

You take the left, I have the right.

Apparently she understood herself, since when she charged forward behind the android, Telisa3 went into action. Her faster duplicate vaulted over a counter and tossed two grenades toward the lasers above before Telisa could even catch up to the android she wanted to use for cover.

Telisa got behind the android and fried it with her breaker claw from point blank range.

Krumpf.

The grenades exploded, sending metal parts flying. The android's body protected Telisa from the shrapnel.

The surviving androids of the checkpoint ran forward to engage them, but the disguises bought them the second they needed.

Blam. Blam, blam, boom.

Telisa3 shot four times before Telisa managed to kill an android with her smart pistol and another with her breaker claw.

Telisa3 started to shoot at spots on the walls and ceiling. Pieces of the base flew through the air in all directions.

Blam, blam, blam.

Sensor stations.

Telisa activated her stealth device. Meanwhile, she heard Telisa3 continue the firefight. Telisa crawled forward out of cover, hoping she was undetectable. Telisa shot a couple targets as they presented themselves, first an android and then a heavier security machine. She noticed something wrong.

The corridor is narrower. It's closing up!

"They're closing it up!" Telisa3 transmitted. "Choose a side, quick!"

"Get ourselves out of here," Telisa said, running for it. "The people here are prisoners, but they're not in any immediate danger."

"Yes. Let's focus on the Trilisks and we can free them later if we win."

The corridor closed behind her. Telisa had not even noticed that aspect of the design earlier; she had assumed the androids and lasers were sufficient obstacles to secure Skyhold.

The Trilisks went to great lengths to make this place secure. Why didn't they just kill the people? Did the prisoners give them authorizations they needed? Leverage?

She followed Telisa3 toward an exterior docking station.

Clear of the entrance strongpoint, Telisa realized she had no ride home. "How did you get here?" she asked.

"Vovokan shuttle," Telisa3 said. "I've summoned it."

Telisa saw from the docking station status monitors that a ship was coming in.

"Can it mate with the dock?"

"Not this one. Quick spacewalk!"

Telisa nodded and told her Veer suit to close up. Her faceplate emerged and covered her head, but it had a hole right over her nose.

"Uh, problem."

"What? Oh," Telisa3 said.

So that's what I look like when I'm thinking hard.

"If I could seal it for just ten seconds," Telisa said.

"Got it," Telisa3 said. "Glue grenade."

"Hrm. Ah. Yes, I guess that works."

"Here, put this over the hole and I'll use the grenade. I'll get you free on the other side." Telisa3 handed her a piece of plastic from a shattered robot panel.

Telisa hesitated.

If you can't trust yourself, woman, you've got issues.

"Okay," Telisa said. She stood over in a corner of the dock station and held the plastic over her faceplate.

"Here goes," Telisa3 sent her over the link. She tossed the grenade at Telisa.

Fooosh! Whump.

Telisa stared at fresh foam as it hardened around her faceplate. Her hand was stuck to her face, too.

"You can breathe?"

"Yes. For now," Telisa said.

"Good, because more androids are here," Telisa3 said.

Blam. Blam. Krumpf.

By the Five.

"Okay, here we go." Telisa3 grabbed her free hand and led her toward the lock. Telisa's link picked up services from the Vovokan shuttle. Her attendants told her it was just outside.

Telisa3 took a minute to get through some safety protocols on the airlock. Telisa's Veer suit was telling the lock computer its integrity had been compromised, making the lock stubborn. Telisa helped things along by getting her suit to shut up. That did not work, so she just re-cloaked using the stealth sphere.

"That'll do it," Telisa3 transmitted. Telisa felt her suit shift subtly as the pressure dropped. Then she was spinning away, but Telisa3 still had a grip on her arm.

Time seemed to pass slowly. Telisa wondered how the other PIT team members had fared, and how many casualties there had been among the Space Force and Earth citizens.

My mission here was an utter failure.

159

Telisa felt the pull of a gravity-spinner stabilized deck beneath her feet. The shuttle showed itself leaving Skyhold in her PV. Then she smelled solvent. Telisa held her breath and waited.

The dried foam blocking her view melted away. When it looked like most of it had cleared away, she closed her eyes and dropped the plastic panel.

Nasty as the solvent smells, it's amazing they managed to get it as close to harmless as they did.

Telisa felt fresh air on her face. She told her faceplate to retract. Telisa saw her duplicate and the inside of a Vovokan shuttle cargo area.

"We made it," Telisa3 said. Telisa saw blood on her arm.

"You got clipped?"

"Yes, my arm. The suit took the brunt of it."

"Let's try to raise Cilreth," Telisa said. She was already trying to open a connection. "Cilreth?"

There was no answer. She tried Jason. The connection went through.

"Telisa! I thought you were dead."

"Quite the opposite. There's two of me here. What's happening?"

"A duplicate? Telisa, I think Shiny's done way too much damage. The Space Force is reporting an all out attack. They say they've taken heavy casualties."

"Of course they're saying that. If it's the Trilisks, they want the populace on their side, hunting for us. If it's just the Space Force, well, they've been expecting an alien attack. Fog of war and all that."

"I'm sorry, Telisa... I don't think they could produce a deception on this grand a scale... the web is filling with endless series of images, messages... CWS has been checking it out. They think it's legitimate. In fact, I'm about five minutes from being arrested here for treason.

The only reason they let me talk to you is probably because they're looking for you."

Telisa opened her mouth to answer when her PV exploded with warning messages.

"Skyhold is breaking up!" Telisa3 blurted from behind her. "It's being destroyed!"

"Telisa! What's that?" Jason asked.

"Skyhold is taking fire. Pieces of it are flying away. I don't see many surviving this," Telisa said.

"Can you pick up survivors?" Jason asked.

"I—"

A bright explosion lit the spacescape. Filters snapped on and cut video feeds from outside the shuttle. More alarms went off.

No one survived that.

"The innocent ones on the list are dead," Telisa said aloud with Jason on the channel. "Plus the Five know how many more."

There was no answer. Telisa's PV showed that the explosion had damaged their communications equipment.

"Cilreth, can you hear me?" Telisa's link routed the request through her attendant sphere.

There was no answer.

"Maintain course and speed," Shiny's voice said. "Planning rendezvous."

"Shiny! By the Five, what's going on?"

Shiny did not answer.

"Shiny!"

Michael McCloskey

Chapter 23

Cilreth struggled to shore up the Clacker against the cyber-attack.

The rogue elements had expanded to a third of *Clacker*'s capacity. Cilreth had launched three iterations of a cleaning program, all of which were running on a subset of the ship's cores. She split her time between writing the next version and managing the ones she had running. The first version had been broken by a counterattack. Thereafter it had made things worse. Cilreth had almost lost control by the time she realized all of the version one programs were pretending to be working but were actually busy doing nothing.

Cilreth kept checking her newer programs. If she spent all her time on the next version, her defense might collapse before she could push it out. She felt a crisis coming on.

I can't do this. I'm losing.

"Hi! What's the situation?" Cilreth2 said, appearing behind her.

Cilreth started, then stood up to yell.

"Where the HELL have you been! Cthulhu awakes! Something has been trying to take over! I half thought it was *you*!"

Cilreth2 lost her smile fast. "I'm on it. Fill me in," she said, settling into a spare chair. She closed her eyes and brought up her Vovokan work PV.

"A pool of resources keeps going rogue. At first it was small and wasn't growing. Hiding. I killed off several batches, then it gave up hiding and went open warfare with me."

"Damn, you're not kidding. Who could it be? Trilisks?"

"Shiny, I think," Cilreth said. "Shiny or Trilisks. Can't be Space Force. Unless it's an AI and it has good inside information."

"Maybe one of the PIT team got captured."

"Work on the next iteration of this," Cilreth said. She passed herself the task. "I'm going to work with what I already have out there."

"Got it. Me to the rescue," Cilreth2 said. Cilreth was too beaten down to appreciate the humorous enthusiasm.

They worked silently for long minutes. Cilreth felt like she held her own at first, then the slide continued. Her only advantage—owning more than half the computing power—was almost gone.

"I found a pattern. The new rogues always appear at the terminus of one of these calls," Cilreth2 said. "We can turn that system off here. I think it might stop the spread."

"Those are supposed to… what? That sinks distributed results into an accumulator?"

"No, it's supposed to prepare to *disperse* tasks across the work group by updating the work cells with the various infrastructure modules needed for each task. In this case, the enemy is riding on that."

"So we can stop it, but it will cost us the ability to deploy new jobs across the worker cells."

"I'll let this one loose, and solve that problem next. We can still deploy jobs as long as they don't need different modules than the old ones, which is restrictive but better than nothing."

Cilreth watched the result. It was slow, but she saw that the enemy stopped growing. Its losses could not be replaced. Cilreth took a huge sigh of relief.

"We have it for now," Cilreth said.

"You said it. For now. Let's see what's going on with our friends," Cilreth2 said. "Wait, what's this? Communications are down."

"The rogues shut them down. I didn't have time—"

"The Space Force is reporting a massive attack, which is expected, but look at these casualty lists. That's a lot more than the suppression Shiny was supposed to be doing."

"Unholy Cthulhu! The *Bismarck*? Skyhold?"

"No way… they must have counted *Bismarck* out because we captured it?" asked Cilreth2.

"It doesn't say missing in action anymore. It says verified destroyed."

"The bug traitored us!"

"Could the Trilisks be making all this up?" asked Cilreth. "After all, they want to galvanize the Space Force against us."

"They were already paranoid about alien attack. It wouldn't take any more galvanization. Also, look at this," Cilreth2 said. She pointed Cilreth at a feed of the Clacker's long range scan of the asteroid belt. It showed massive changes in moving objects in the belt. Cilreth looked at the largest differences. Each was a large asteroid where a Space Force base had been located. Those asteroids had been broken into millions of pieces.

"You're right. And the tracking system is showing only *five percent* of Terran military traffic we registered upon arrival."

"Is there any chance the rogue elements introduced this? Are we still hacked and don't know it?"

"Well there are *Trilisks* around. Who knows what they could do?" Cilreth pointed out.

"No. You know what? The Trilisks of old would just take over the whole ship in a heartbeat. This was Shiny's doing. Magnus was right all along."

"What can we do?" Cilreth said.

"Attack the big bug back. We have the *Clacker*."

"He's got several…"

"We know which one he's in. If we're lucky, maybe we get him. Or take out his Trilisk AI."

Cilreth nodded. "Okay. You've got offense. Target him. I'll see to our defenses."

It's easy to agree with myself, even on the radical ideas.

Cilreth diverted power to the defenses of the massive starship. She kept one eye out for the cyber attack to return. Part of her thought its demise was too good to be true.

Maybe I finally plugged all the holes Shiny can use to get in.

Vovokan ship to ship weapons were mostly energy-based. Cilreth fed the Clacker's EM shields to a large power reserve and put the ship on an erratic course. Since the other ships were farther than a light minute away, having an erratic course could help to avoid counter attacks.

Cilreth saw the ship's energy reserve drop in half.

"Salvo away," Cilreth2 said. "We'll see what Shiny thinks of that!"

Cilreth waited nervously. It would be a while before they could discern results. The round trip for light all the way out to the belt would ensure that.

"Cilreth?" It was Jason.

"Yes Jason. What news?"

"Well we fried several Trilisks, but Vovokan ships have been wiping out the Space Force."

"I know. We've attacked Shiny. But it's just the *Clacker* against all the others."

"If you can point out the location of the other ships, I can pass that along," Jason said.

"I'll send you their last known locations," Cilreth said. She sent Jason the pointer.

"Have you heard from the rest of the team?" Jason asked.

"No, but our computers were attacked. We lost communications for a long while."

"I say contact them directly," Cilreth2 said. "We have to disconnect. I think this link traffic could help Shiny pinpoint our location and hit us."

"Good luck," Jason said, then disconnected.

The other Vovokan ships in the system flickered then disappeared from the system scan.

"I'd like to say that means you got them, but since you shot at one and they all disappeared, it just means he's alerted to our hostility."

"R'lyeh rising! They're coming for us!"

"Did that damn centipede betray us or was he taken over by Trilisks?"

The *Clacker* shook violently.

"What's that? There's no way he could have returned fire so quickly!" Cilreth said.

"*Returned* fire, no. Maybe he *already* fired before ours got there."

"I took evasives."

"We need to modify our algorithms. Also, who knows what those rogues accomplished?"

"That took most of our reserve," Cilreth said. She checked the damage report. It became clear they had been hit by more than one ship. "Three of them! We're fighting three of them. And they're closer than we thought."

"If we can take one out, it could mean a lot for Terra."

The ship shook again.

"We're being hit again!"

The energy reserves drained to zero. The *Clacker* shuddered more violently. Cilreth watched giant pieces start to break off the ship in her PV. Massive explosions ripped through the remains and flickered out quickly in the vacuum. The deck under them just kept shaking. The artificial gravity went dead.

"That shuttle," Cilreth2 said. "You go now. You know I can catch up." She pointed out an escape ship on their ship map.

"You better," Cilreth said, clumsily releasing herself from her seat. She called for attendants to help pull her to the escape vessel.

I'm not equipped for this. I don't have my pack. Not even a flashlight.

Cilreth hoped there still would be a shuttle there when she arrived.

Chapter 24

"He has us," Telisa3 announced.

The *Thumper* held Telisa's shuttle in an invisible grip. It drew them in for docking.

"He wasn't supposed to be anywhere near this close to Earth," Telisa pointed out.

"Really? I still don't know most of the plan. For instance, I suppose I'm headed back to stasis soon?"

"I don't know," Telisa said.

Telisa's mind had been racing. Was Jason seeing the data fed to Earth as part of a Trilisk deception to rally the populace against what should be their liberators? Or had Shiny actually ruthlessly attacked Earth?

There is so much of it. So many dead. He must have switched to competition mode. The lure of a whole system of his own was more valuable than our alliance.

Telisa felt sick. If it was true...

The massive Vovokan ship consumed the tiny shuttle and brought it into a massive bay. Then, the lock cycled and the doors opened.

"Here's where we get off," Telisa3 said nervously.

Telisa walked side by side with her double down the ramp. They walked onto a huge bay floor, looking for Shiny. Nothing moved. The openings of dozens of Vovokan caves beckoned from several levels adjoining the bay.

Reality flickered. It was almost not noticeable.

"What just happened?" Telisa said. She flinched. Telisa3 was gone. Telisa checked her link.

"You there? Did you stealth?"

There was no answer.

"What? What's wrong?" even as she asked, she realized she suddenly had memories of Telisa3, walking up in a column room and getting instructions from Shiny. Then she had flown to Skyhold, alone and nervous, worrying about the lack of information. She had actually been glad to meet her original, because it made her feel better about going into a situation on Shiny's word alone.

We're synced up. Telisa3 will know about Magnus now. She's probably inside a Trilisk column.

"Why did you sync us up?" Telisa sent the question to Shiny.

Finally the alien answered her. "Telisa duplicate not meant, intended, planned to survive mission."

That's not a good start.

"Tell me what's happening," Telisa said.

"Trilisks neutralized. Shiny taking control. Cooperation no longer optimal."

"You attacked the Space Force? Our plan was to distract them and minimize casualties."

"Shiny taking control. Space Force damaged, crippled, disabled. Terrans subservient, dependent, enslaved to Shiny."

It's all true.

Telisa fell to her knees, overwhelmed. Her worst case scenario was true. Shiny had betrayed them, and killed huge numbers of people doing it. A huge proportion of the blame fell upon Telisa.

"The *Bismarck*?" she dared ask.

"Terran battleship destroyed in attempt to escape, elude, evade," Shiny reported.

At least Magnus didn't live to see his fears were warranted. He could saying 'I told you so' about now, her inner monologue said. But Telisa knew he would never have said it. He would try and fix it. Still, it took her a long moment to continue.

"Shiny. I want to negotiate a release of my race. We will pay you handsomely. Serve you in many ways. But total servitude takes away all hope from us. We won't accomplish as much under your heel as we can on our own. Terrans do not function optimally when forced to serve. We want cooperation, not competition. We're not Vovokans."

"Understood. Cooperation not optimal at this time. Other deal, bargain, arrangement is possible. Shiny delineate, explain, propose?"

Hopelessness assailed Telisa. She was perhaps the greatest traitor Terra had ever known. And Magnus... so long gone.

I want to die.

"Go on," she said, though her voice broke.

"Telisa copy departs, flees, leaves Earth. Shiny controls Earth. Telisa forbidden interference, resistance, defiance. Telisa copy collects artifacts. Give, submit, provide artifacts to Shiny. Comply for period of ten Earth years, Shiny returns Magnus copy to Telisa."

"What! You have Magnus? Where is he?" Telisa exploded. She jumped to her feet.

"Trilisk column set aside. Column contains Magnus data. Possible to create Magnus clone. This is offered compensation for surrender, compliance, obedience."

"Which one? Where is it!" Telisa sent queries from her link to ship's services. The *Thumper* denied her access.

"Consider, contemplate, evaluate offer," Shiny said.

"If you're worried about my resistance, why don't you just kill me, like you did to those thousands of Space Force men and women?" Telisa asked bitterly.

"Telisa useful, skilled, beneficial. Known quantity. Shiny will not kill, destroy, eliminate unless optimal. Space Force threat removed, eliminated, destroyed with minimum loss of life."

Minimum? The minimum in this case is very high.

"You deceived us all," Telisa said. Tears began to stream down her face. "You've lost your trust forever. Prove to me he's still alive. Show me. Make him."

"Not optimal for Shiny at this time."

"He is my motivation. I won't serve you without proof. I refuse your deal."

Shiny did not answer.

I believed in him. I won't ever do it again.

Telisa waited for a minute, wondering what would happen next. Finally, her link received a pointer. She accessed it, causing a green routing line to appear. She followed it.

Maybe he revived Magnus.

Telisa started to run. Past the first door, the floor was covered in sand. The inside of the *Thumper* held only dark Vovokan caverns. Telisa ran on desperately. She slipped in the sand, struggled to get up, then kept going.

The route led deeper into the ship. Part of her worried about a trap for a second, but she dismissed it. Things could not get any worse. Telisa's hope soared when she saw a square, sand-free room with Trilisk columns. She staggered forward, dropping grains of sand all over the floor. Then she saw him.

Magnus. Telisa did not care which copy he was.

He looked confused. Telisa ran into his arms.

"Hello?" he said.

"You were right about Shiny. He took over Earth. You're dead. I mean, the first you is dead and I think the second one is, too. You were made from a Trilisk column."

Magnus4 held her tighter.

"I see things are getting complicated. I'm confused of course. I don't even know *when* I am. If that's true… Telisa, listen to me. You have to run away. I'll cover your escape. Find someplace safe, then figure out what to do about Shiny."

"He says he'll let you live free again if I don't interfere for ten years," Telisa said.

"Can we escape this place?"

"No. We're on his ship. He has control of everything."

"You can't serve him for ten years. He might not let me go, anyway."

"I will. That's what I intend to do. I'll figure out how to make sure it's in Shiny's best interest to release you. Then I'll have you again."

Magnus4 pushed her back and looked into her teary face.

"I think you could accomplish that. But what damage can he do in the meantime? He'll solidify his hold over Terra. That's why he wants time."

Telisa shook her head. "I know it's selfish but I don't care. I have to have you back. I *have* to. I'm not strong enough alone. With you, I know we could do anything."

"Think it over when your head clears," he said. "In a few days, you'll see it differently. Investigate your options, just in case. I've lived a fantastic life. You don't need to sacrifice Earth to get me back."

But there's nothing I can do anyway.

She nodded. "I'll think about it every day."

They embraced one last time before reality skipped a beat again, stealing him away.

***

Telisa3 awakened inside a Trilisk column. The last clear tube receded into the floor allowing her to exit. She tested her strength, leaping high into the air.

That's what I thought. I'm the copy now. Well, I've always been the copy, but now I have the memories of the original. The meeting with Magnus. I'm supposed to go out and work for Shiny.

The alien summoned her to another part of the ship. She followed a mental lane indicator. It led out of the room and into a sand-filled tunnel.

I'm on the Thumper.

As she walked back, surrounded by the odd caverns preferred by Vovokans, her sorrow started to channel into anger. But she was thoughtful.

Shiny won't free us unless it's in his best interest to do so. I have to defeat him, or blackmail him. Offer him something he needs.

The tears came again, but only for a minute. She had better control by the time she came to report to the alien. When she appeared before Shiny, or a Shiny copy, the alien gave her a status report on the PIT team.

"*Clacker* destroyed," Shiny said. "One Cilreth captured. Other PIT team members survive: Imanol, Siobhan, Caden, Jason."

"And the original me. And Magnus."

"Magnus not available, usable, assigned for your next mission, undertaking, objective," Shiny said.

"I'll be more effective with Magnus. You still have our homeworld."

"Shiny offer delineated, explained, proposed."

"The others will work for you? Are you blackmailing them, too?"

"Others obey, work, listen to Telisa," Shiny said. "Telisa prepared? Target world selected, chosen, planned."

Telisa3 stared at Shiny with a look of raw hatred. Her cheeks glistened with moisture from her tears.

"I'm ready," she said.

Made in the USA
Monee, IL
24 November 2020